Calbraith B. Perry

Twelve Years Among the Colored People

A record of the work of Mount Calvary chapel of S. Mary the Virgin, Baltimore

Calbraith B. Perry

Twelve Years Among the Colored People
A record of the work of Mount Calvary chapel of S. Mary the Virgin, Baltimore

ISBN/EAN: 9783337288563

Printed in Europe, USA, Canada, Australia, Japan

Cover: Foto ©Andreas Hilbeck / pixelio.de

More available books at **www.hansebooks.com**

TWELVE YEARS

AMONG

THE COLORED PEOPLE.

A RECORD OF THE WORK OF MOUNT CALVARY
CHAPEL OF S. MARY THE VIRGIN,
BALTIMORE.

BY

CALBRAITH B. PERRY,

PRIEST IN CHARGE.

NEW YORK:

JAMES POTT & CO.,

12 ASTOR PLACE.

1884.

PREFACE.

THE following pages were begun during a few weeks of enforced rest from active labor, in response to repeated requests from friends, benefactors and fellow-workers for information respecting the methods adopted in carying on the work of St. Mary's Chapel. It was hoped that by a brief history of the work the information could be more satisfactorily given than was possible by private correspondence. To the fulfillment of this purpose it was sought to add such details as would make a permanent record prized by the colored people who have been associated with the parish. In carrying out this very restricted and simple purpose, the review of difficulties of the past, the singular perplexities of the present, and the great uncertainty of the whole problem of the future of the colored people, have tempted the writer to extend the plan, and to offer some suggestions, and to draw some inferences from a somewhat exceptional experience, which he trusts will not be wholly unacceptable nor unprofitable to such readers as may be induced by their interest in the subject to consider them.

In performing the task, it was impossible not to foresee that in the endeavor to tell the whole truth and to express his opinions with entire candor, he would hardly escape wounding the feelings and perhaps call forth some earnest, if not bitter, dissent alike from the people of the North, of the South, and from the colored people themselves. But he felt no less convinced that it was only by telling the truth and the whole truth that he could contribute testimony of any value in the solution of a problem of great difficulties doubtless, but of still greater importance. He has long since learned that he can rely upon the indulgence of his friends for all errors of judgment, many of which will doubtless be detected in these pages. A more general public he does not venture to hope to reach. For defects of any other character his only apology must be that he makes no pretension to a right to enroll himself on the too-crowded list of authors, other than an intimate knowledge of the things of which he writes.

THE AUTHOR.

MOUNT CALVARY CLERGY HOUSE,
 Nov. 1*st*, 1884.

CONTENTS.

TWELVE YEARS AMONG THE COLORED PEOPLE.

CHAPTER I.

INTRODUCTORY.

THE work among the colored people at Mount Calvary Chapel of S. Mary the Virgin, began in the year 1873. Some reference to the events of the three years preceding is necessary in order to explain the writer's connection with it. The cloud under which he began his work will account for obstacles and annoyances which will appear later in the record. These it is important to recognize and to distinguish from difficulties necessarily connected with labors among the colored people. They will also serve to show that no political or sectional motive led him to labor among them. The fierce and protracted struggle through which he entered the ministry may also furnish a sort of *apologia pro vita sua*, and account for what may have been in his earlier years an unnecessary aggressiveness and harshness in pressing principles which he holds no whit less firmly to-day but, he trusts, with more gentleness and a wider charity to those who differ from him.

7

Unable to obtain Priest's Orders in the diocese
where he had begun his labors,* at the invitation of
Bishop Whittingham and Vestry of Mount Calvary

* In justice to himself the writer adds an explanation of
the cause of his ordination being postponed in Rhode Island.
He had been censured for certain expressions in a sermon
upon the Doctrine of the Real Presence. The sermon was
presented as a mere seminary exercise. The statements,
though perhaps unguarded and crude, and characteristic
of an undergraduate, were pronounced by eminent and
strictly conservative divines to be defensible. But in addition to this alleged offense he was soon after with a number
of his classmates in "Retreat" making preparation for his
approaching ordination. Retreats (seasons of united prayer
and meditation), now quite familiar to the Church and
countenanced by many of our bishops, were then ranked
among the "novelties that disturbed our peace." The
then Dean of the Seminary, who, as Dr. Mahan cleverly
expressed it, had changed his ecclesiastical coat so frequently as to be suspicious of the loyalty of others, sent a
sensational telegram to several of the bishops in regard to
their candidates. In dioceses such as Albany and New
York little effect was produced ; but in Rhode Island, a
"Retreat" was regarded with horror proportionate to the
ignorance of its nature. The rector of the old parish
church by which the writer had been recommended to
the Standing Committee, refused his signature to the
required testimonials, and the majority of the Vestry requested the withdrawal of their signatures which had
been already given. Several, however, refused to join in
the narrow policy, and remained his steadfast friends.
But for the ever-liberal and kind-hearted character of
the Bishop of Rhode Island, and the persistent mediation
of Prof. Seymour (now Bishop of Springfield), who had
come to Rhode Island to present the candidates for ordina-

Church he became Associate Rector of that church. Having received warning from Rhode Island against so dangerous a refugee, and already suspicious and irritated by the perversion of the late Rector of Mount Calvary to the Church of Rome, the Standing Committee of Maryland made a condition of the writer's receiving ordination that he should pass an examination before the Bishop in the presence of a special and extra-canonical commission of clergy.

It was a formidable ordeal for a young deacon. He well remembers the impressive form of the venerable Bishop of Maryland, surrounded by seven prominent clergy of his diocese, and the fiery, yet kindly glance of the eye beaming with the encouragement which he so frequently gathered from the same look in after years. Nor can he forget the five weary hours of inquisition. Its history does not properly belong to these pages. Before taking

tion, his ordination to the diaconate would probably not have been obtained at that time. At the expiration of a year, his ordination to the priesthood seemed hopelessly postponed. The Associate Mission in Providence, of which the present Rector of Mount Calvary was the head, was disbanded, Mr. Coggeshall (the late Father Coggeshall, S.S.J.E.), removed to the more liberal Diocese of New Jersey, and the writer, although much attached to his little flock at S. Gabriel's, and to a bishop in whose family he had enjoyed a son's privilege and intercourse, at length yielded to the persuasions of his old friend Mr. Richey to accept the Associate Rectorship of Mount Calvary Church, Baltimore, where the hearty welcome of Bishop Whittingham had been assured him.

leave of that group of doctors of divinity, however,—some of them since. become dear friends of the writer, and none, he trusts, his enemies—it may not be uninteresting to describe the closing scene. After hours of ferreting for hidden heresies, the crucial point of Sacramental Confession was reached. The deacon was asked if he felt at liberty to use any form of private absolution, and if so, what form. He replied that while feeling himself at liberty in private ministration to use any form connected with the teachings of our Church, he should use that in the English Prayer Book. Upon the expression of disapprobation of several of the clergy, the bishop, bending forward, asked in his eager way: "Do you remember, Perry, anything in the preface of our Prayer Book that proves your right to do so?" In reply the words were given : "This Church is far from intending to depart from the Church of England in any essential point of doctrine, discipline or worship." "Right!" exclaimed the bishop, falling back in evident satisfaction. Dr. Dalrymple, whose jovial face, beaming with suppressed merriment, is not chiefly associated with the work of an inquisitor, then asked :

"Does it seem of no significance that that form was omitted from our Prayer Book ?" Without leaving time for reply, the bishop interrupted with vehemence: "Dr. Dalrymple, by the principle your question implies, you would make of our Church nothing but a miserable Protestant sect."

He then related how, when a Unitarian minister
called on him to ask the terms upon which he
could enter the Church's ministry, he took from
his shelves an English Prayer Book and read him
the Athanasian Creed.   This did not convince the
doctor.   He pressed the deacon further till the
bishop again came to the rescue, while the ex-
hausted deacon sank back glad of a respite.   " Dr.
Dalrymple, let me tell you what happened in the
earlier years of my ministry.   A man came to me
bowed down with the weight of a great sin.   I
used those ' Comfortable Words ' that you have
recommended to Mr. Perry to use under such circumstances, but these and similar promises did
not comfort him.   Then I said, Kneel down, and as
in the presence of God, acknowledge your sin.   He
did so, and I stood up and repeated over him those
words that you have condemned in this young
man.   Now, Dr. Dalrymple, did I do right, or
did I do wrong ? "   The doctor replied that he
was not sitting in judgment upon his bishop.   The
bishop insisted on an answer.   Dr. D. said with
some spirit, " Bishop, you invited me to assist in
examining this young man—you have turned the
occasion into one of examining me ! "   Still the
bishop insisted ; by this time those who knew him
will fancy the color of the good doctor's face and
bald head.   He seized the generous brimmed hat
from the floor, and while he rapidly polished with the
silk handkerchief which he drew from it, his head,
which now glowed like an inverted caldron heated

in the furnace, he said as he half rose, "Bishop, if you insist upon my answering, I shall leave the house." "Just as you please," said the undaunted bishop ; "but I wish an answer before you go." This was too much, and the doctor blurted out, "Well, bishop, if you insist, I think you did wrong." A scathing rejoinder followed on the part of the bishop, which cannot be recalled, but it was the final single combat of the battle, and soon after, when the deacon had retired for half an hour and had been readmitted, it was announced to him that the majority of the clergy had expressed an opinion in favor of Ordination. It is but justice to add that, before leaving the house, Dr. Dalrymple approached the writer and said : "My young brother, I do not think you ought to be in the ministry and I have done all I could to keep you out. But my brethren here think differently. I have discharged my duty. Now give me your hand, and promise me that since you are to be ordained we shall be good friends." The dear, honest old man faithfully kept the agreement, and many a pleasant invitation was afterward given, and, when possible, accepted, while he was one of the most generous and ready contributors to the work at S. Mary's. Would that all the brethren had taken the same generous, genial course !

The bishop, having announced the decision of the clergy, rose, and, with an earnest, searching look in his eagle eyes, said : "And now I shall have to ask you the same question I require to be an-

swered by all whom I ordain : Do you accept the
XXXIX Articles in their plain, grammatical, but "
—and, pausing, he threw out, in his emphatic way,
his long index finger—"their historical sense?"
On receiving a ready assent, he brought his hands
together, exclaiming, "Thank God, thank God!"

The intimate intercourse with the Episcopal
household, which was a privilege from that day ;
the tender, fatherly counsel, the sympathy in
trouble, the frequent guidance in many little details of parish work, would appear improbable to
those who only have heard the Mount Calvary
clergy described as arrayed against the bishop.
These relations will be understood better by those
who knew how loving and true and kind the
bishop could be to those whom he felt it necessary, at times, to rebuke more sharply, and to condemn more strongly than those for whom he felt
less responsibility.

On one occasion one of many requests had been
made by the Bishop about details of ritual at Mount
Calvary and S. Mary's. This time it was that none
other but black or white stoles should be used.
Other churches of the city, without let or hinder-
ance, were using the other ecclesiastical colors. A
promise of obedience was given, but not without
the suggestion that it seemed a little hard to be re-
strained from such slight excesses of ritual when
there were other churches by omission violating so
many rubrics and canons. "Well, Perry," replied
the bishop, with a smile, "what is the use of be-

lieving in bishops if you are not ready to suffer for your principles ? If I should interfere with the practices of S. —— "—mentioning a typical Low Church parish—" they would not obey me."

Those who, ignorant of the true relations with the bishop, have represented the clergy of Mount Calvary as ruthlessly delighting in tormenting their bishop, have utterly failed to appreciate the delicate position in which the clergy found themselves. . They came into the diocese when, as he saw his eventful episcopate drawing to its close, the bishop shrank from meeting, with enfeebled powers, fresh conflicts. Yet while he strove to avoid collision, when called to act, with his old intrepidity he spared neither himself nor others in fulfilling the duty. Some who saw him painfully rise to vindicate himself in that convention, when he had been presented by priests of his own diocese for trial, recalled the dignity and indomitable courage, mingled with anguish, of Thorwaldsen's Dying Lion.

Mount Calvary Church, to which these clergy, but lately from the seminary, were called, was also in a critical condition. An idolized rector—deservedly esteemed—but whose work had been peculiarly, we might add, unfortunately, personal, had deserted to the Roman Church. It was commonly reported that many of the congregation were about to follow their former guide. Many, certainly, were naturally distressed and disturbed. It is believed that only seven communicants, all of them women, were lost to our communion. But sudden changes in teaching or ritual, even had the clergy desired them, might have produced disastrous results.

The welfare of their flock pressed upon the hearts of these young and inexperienced clergy no less than consideration and reverence for their father in God. They had reason to know that many things, although some were personally distasteful to the Bishop, would not have called forth censure but for intense pressure from without. They knew from himself that in most important points he sympathized with them—that, as he himself expressed it, he disliked only the fringes of a work which otherwise he heartily approved. Under these circumstances some differences were inevitable. To those who knew the strong, fiery, dogmatic natures of those great, generous souls, Bishop Whittingham's and Joseph Richey's, it is a proof of the considerateness of both that in nearly all points, after the first moments of heat, a loving agreement was reached. The interference on the part of a bishop in such minute details of ritual, such as material of the vestments, the distinction between the color of the ornamentation and the groundwork of a stole, and the like, would have been resented by many of the clergy who accused Richey of a refractory spirit; but to Richey his bishop was a father, with much higher claims upon him than that derived from canons. The bishop also freely acknowledged that he directed in matters which he did not seek to regulate in other churches. For this there were several reasons. His own relationship to the parish from the first had been most intimate ; Mount Calvary was spoken of as the bishop's church ; he and his family attended its services. He himself alludes to another reason in a letter to Richey : " Painful facts, daily coming to my knowledge, in illustration of the evil results of ' letting alone ' your predecessor in the course so disastrously pursued by him." But perhaps the chief cause was that Mount Calvary was made the center of attack by a school of churchmanship that had battled with him throughout his Episcopate. It was his wish, at whatever cost except that of principle, to avoid occasion for further conflict. In cases where personal preferences alone were concerned the Mount Calvary clergy were repeatedly yielding to his wishes. On one occasion the daily press had, without any foundation whatever, announced the "blessing" of the new altar of Mount Calvary, and also referred to the disuse of the Processional Cross on the occasion of an Episcopal visitation. This, brought to his official notice, called forth a formal and formidable letter from the Bishop forbidding the clergy severally and individually from any blessing of the altar, as it had led him to suppose that either they were about to arrogate Episcopal functions by blessing it themselves, or had committed schism by inviting some other Bishop to intrude into his diocese, since, he added with amusing irony, he had no reason to suppose the services of his assistant bishop had been secured. He also requested the discontinuance of the "gestatory cross." Without a moment's hesitation, Mr. Richey briefly replied in the name of the clergy that the bishop might rest assured that had the thought of blessing the altar been entertained, which was not the case, he would have been asked to officiate, and that the use of the "Processional Cross," at his request would be discontinued. It seemed as if the note could have barely reached the Episcopal residence when the brief reply was received: "Dear Brethren: You have rejoiced the heart of your bishop and fulfilled his highest expectation of you. Your loving friend and brother, WILLIAM R. WHITTINGHAM, Bishop of Maryland." The matter which unhappily embittered the last days of the bishop and caused so much sorrow to the clergy of Mount Calvary in inflicting pain upon him in their stead while they were helpless to relieve him, was of a different nature. In discontinuing the use of the Commendatory Prayer at funerals, a custom of several clergy of the Diocese at the time and of not a few of other Dioceses, it at first seemed to them that they were asked to yield truth which they were bound to defend. But as soon as the bishop, with that skill which was a chief element of his greatness, so placed the matter that obedience could be given without the wounding of consciences over-sensitive in the estimate of some, but which he respected, the clergy with

2

alacrity yielded. With characteristic delicacy the Bishop wrote : " By looking again at my letter of the 24th, you will perceive that it is an expression of regret for ' offense ' 'afforded '—not *committed* —and therefore in the nature of expostulation and warning—not of censure or disciplinary admonition." Removing all difficulty in acceding to his wish by the ground upon which he placed it, he added : " No doctrinal point is in discussion, but a rule of practice, and that not of private, personal practice, but of the public official practice of one exercising a trust under authority." Had others shown a like wise, tender and conciliatory spirit, the judicial archives of the Church would not now be disfigured with a record at once cruel, ignorant and unjust. The disagreements of the clergy of Mount Calvary with their bishop were published on the housetops. The affectionate personal relations of which we have spoken could not then be made known. However the bishop may have spoken to them or of them in moments of irritation, he ever continued to affectionately urge them to remain at their posts in his Diocese.

When Mr. Richey told him of his acceptance of a very honorable position in the Faculty of a College, and his proposed resignation of Mount Calvary, he replied that he took the responsibility of forbidding him to leave the Diocese, as he could not spare him. Mr. Richey submitted without a murmur, though at great sacrifice to himself, and then, contrary to his judgment and inclination.

Bishop Whittingham did not use language care-
lessly ; yet in a letter, dated August 28, 1877, he
thus sanctions the work which will be the subject
of these pages, speaking of its " remarkable degree
of good success": "In my long experience I
have known none more signal, and in my judgment complete, as regards both spiritual and tem-
poral." "Under Mr. Perry it has my entire confidence."

It might be of more questionable delicacy to
dwell upon the delight of family intercourse in
the bishop's household permitted to the young
clergy, especially while living as near neighbors.
The pleasure, however, cannot be resisted of recall-
ing the morning when the saintly De Koven, calling with the Rector of S. Paul's on the Mount
Calvary clergy, found the writer very ill. Ascend-
ing the stairs to his sick-room, he met that dear
and well-loved partner of the Bishop's joys and
sorrows on the stairs with a tray. " Why, Mrs.
Whittingham, how came you here ?" said the
Warden of Racine. "Oh," replied the kind
friend, "I am just coming down from giving a
luncheon which I bring every day to my boy."
" Why ! is your son here ?" inquired the Doctor.
"These young clergy are my boys," explained
the dear friend who for days had prepared with
her own hands and brought to his bedside little
delicacies to tempt the appetite of the convalescent. When he recovered, the bishop sent a
large yellow silk handkerchief, which he strictly

charged his young clergyman to wear as a protection to his throat, when he first officiated in church. It was with great glee he informed the Bishop that the latter was guilty of "introducing ritualistic novelties, as there was much excitement at a 'gold amice' having been worn at Morning Prayer!"

It is hoped that these anecdotes of one whose life, even with the delightful and just record that a dear friend has written of it, cannot be too well known, will excuse what might otherwise seem foreign to the purpose in hand. If not, let it be permitted as a tribute of justice and affection to a loved and lamented bishop, and to a dear brother priest, whose memories are among the writer's dearest treasures of the past. It is believed, also, that the knowledge of those earlier events will not be useless in forming a right estimate of much which will follow in these pages.

CHAPTER II.

SOON after coming to Baltimore, the writer was
asked to conduct a service in S. Philip's Mission.
This little congregation of colored people wor-
shiped in a small hall over a feed-store on Howard street. The Opera House now occupies the
site. The room gave evidence of care and an attempt at reverence, yet it was cheerless in the ex-
treme. On one side was a large tank, used as a
font by a former pastor, an eccentric clergyman,
afterward by times a member of the Oriental
Church and a Baptist. The small altar had once
been a shopkeeper's counter. An altar frontal
spoke of loving hands but poverty of resources.
On this absurdly diminutive altar were two tiny
candlesticks. They were not even as large as
those carried by a prominent New York rector in
his pocket to his church, who in reply to the pro-
test of a brother clergyman that they were ridicu-
lously out of proportion to the spacious building,
said quietly : "They will grow." They have
grown. Between these candlesticks was a black
walnut cross as large as the altar. As it was the

gift of Dr. Milo Mahan, it has been carved and gilded, and returned to S. Mary's, out of loving reverence for the lamented donor. It appears large on the present altar, which is ten times the size of the little one at S. Philip's.

But these peculiarities were forgotten, when the service began, in the enjoyment of the hearty responses, the sweet music, the reverence, the unostentatious yet ardent earnestness of the people. The enjoyment was not seriously interrupted even by the rats which ran about the floor during the service. In this cheerless room, amid great discouragements, these colored folks had loyally and persistently maintained services, though frequently for months at a time without the presence of a clergyman. At such times one of their number acted as Lay reader, and the parish visiting, care of the sick and relief of the poor were systematically divided among the communicants. One of these Lay readers is now the Rev. James Thompson, successfully working in Chicago. He had been ordained before we first knew S. Philip's. Another is the Rev. C. M. C. Mason of St. Louis. Of his earnest work among his people in that city the Bishop of Missouri and clergy of St. Louis have spoken in strongest terms. Mr. Mason, after the breaking up of S. Philip's, became one of the most active workers in S. Mary's, and to the lovely Christian example of his wife, the daughter of our Senior Warden, Mr. W. H. Bishop, and to her energy as organist and choir trainer, S. Mary's owes much of the success of her earlier years. On the death of his wife, Mr. Mason moved to St. Louis and assisted his old friend Mr. Thompson. When the latter accepted a call to Chicago, Mr. Mason, strongly urged by the bishop, received Holy Orders and became rector of the vacant parish.

An extract from a communication of Mr. Mason to the *Monthly Chronicle,* a paper published in the interest of the colored people in the earlier years of our work, will best relate the end of S. Philip's.

After describing the starting out of S. Philip's mission in the year 1868, from the older congregation of S. James', whose existence at that time he writes, " might have been considered precarious owing to the sad neglect they were treated with by the churches in this city," the letter gives an account of obtaining the consent of Bishop Whittingham to hold services, and of his placing the infant mission under the charge of the Rev. A. A. Curtis of Mount Calvary Church. It is singular that they should have had this early connection with the church in which they were to find a home in after years. The Rev. W. D. Martin, now of Eastport, Maine, but then one of the vestry of Mount Cavalry Church, acted as their lay reader. Then follows the history of several years' struggle under various missionaries, after which the letter proceeds as follows :

" We had received notice that the building in which we had erected our chapel had been sold to the city and would shortly pass into its hands; not being able to secure another in the neighborhood, and with the countenance of our friends turned from us, our days as a congregation seemed numbered. Mr. Maitland, a lay reader who had often been with us, thinking to cheer us in our trouble, got several clergymen, among them the Rev. Fleming James and Rev. Hugh Roy Scott, to come down at about the last service held at our chapel. Mr. James preached. He took for his text, Ex. xiv. 15, "Speak to the children of Israel that they go forward." There was a great deal to cheer in the sermon,—there would have been more if we could have known just then who was *our* Moses. Immediately after the service we appointed a committee to wait upon the rectors of the churches who heretofore had assisted us to see if any of them would take us in charge. The committee, at a following meeting, reported that all those waited upon had expressed for various reasons their inability to do so, except the rector of Mount Calvary (Rev. Joseph Richey), who said if a hall could not be obtained, he would make provision in his church, even to the extent of a special service should we desire it; *though all the pews were free to all who chose to come, at any and every service.*

On Sunday, May 11, 1873, the Missionary congregation of S. Philip's was dissolved. On Sunday, May 18, the people who composed it identified themselves with Mount Calvary Chapel of S. Mary the

Virgin. It is a little singular to remark that the sermon preached at the first service (11 o'clock A.M.) by the Rev. Mr. Perry, priest in charge, was from the same text in Exodus that the Rev. F. James took for his; it caused some of us to think that we had found our Moses. At the evening service the rector of the parish, Rev. Joseph Richey, preached. In the course of his remarks, in stating why they expected to succeed in a work that others had so signally failed in, he said, "We have given you an altar no whit inferior to that in the parish church ; your services shall be the counterpart of those in Mount Calvary, and everything that is necessary for the edification of the people there, its likeness shall be given you." We were treated no longer as outcasts to whom it should be considered a sufficient favor if the smallest trifle was given, but as children of One Father, bought by the Blood of One Redeemer, and sanctified by One Holy Spirit."

And so the work has been successful, was so the moment those utterances were given with the determination to act upon them.

Mr. Smith, the bishop's secretary—now the Rev. J. Stewart Smith—often acted as lay reader at S. Philip's, and it was at his suggestion that the delegation called on the Mount Calvary Clergy whom he had already interested in the cause.

The senior member of this committee, Mr. Richard Mason, a veteran in church work, frankly confessed that the city clergy had warned them against "Ritualism," and that it would not be

to their advantage to connect themselves with
Mount Calvary Church, "but," he naïvely added,
"we have called in vain on these clergy to help
us. What can we do but come to you?"

The lion-hearted Richey was not the man to
turn a deaf ear to such an appeal, however lim-
ited his resources. While his invitation to the
colored congregation to attend the services of
Mount Calvary was heartily appreciated—the italics
in the above letter are Mr. Mason's—they strongly
urged that their separate existence should be maintained and a place of worship provided.

They undoubtedly were right. However much
any distinction in God's house or at God's altar as
to race, color or condition is to be condemned, it is
practically necessary, at least for the present, that
the Church should extend among the colored people chiefly by getting them into separate congregations, or where that is not possible, by holding
special services for them.

It is said that, at the North, offerings are with-
held on the plea that the negroes to-day are as
much the parishioners of the Southern clergy as
are the whites, and that therefore there is no need
of incurring expense by furnishing for them special clergy and churches. This is pure "theory."

The writer speaks as a Northerner, an "unre-
constructed" Northerner, and as an advocate of
the colored man. Yet he is bound to acknowledge
that he finds quite as much genuine attachment to
the colored man in the South as in the North. If

in the South there be a more deep-seated feeling about the negro's social equality, right of suffrage, and his mingling with white people in schools, hotels, and public conveyances, there is much less feeling of personal aversion to him on account of color than in the North. Only those who 'have lived in both sections of the country can rightly comprehend this difference, or perhaps fully believe in its existence.

Southerners have grown up with them as play-mates or foster-brothers to whom they are tenderly attached, and do not scruple to show marks of strong affection. Old household servants bear relations to their former masters and mistresses which are utterly unknown in Northern households. Even those closer relations of blood, which form the dark-est and foulest feature in the history of slavery, are not without examples of the love that would nat-urally spring from such relationship.

Southerners would resent dining with colored people as fellow-guests at a hotel or restaurant, or even sharing a seat in the railway car, unless they traveled as servants with them. We have known ladies who would have struck from their visiting list a friend who entertained a colored guest, even the most cultured, but in times of lone-liness or illness would share their bed with their old "Mammy" without hesitation. The events of the last twenty-five years have greatly disturbed those relations, yet among the old Southern fami-lies there remains much of the former tenderness, well illustrated by an anecdote of a Southern bishop often related to the writer by this bishop's dear friend, himself a representative Southerner, and which we give in the words in which he has written it out for us.

"Only one personally familiar with what has ceased—thank God!—knows how many were the checks to a master's power, and how many the counterpoises to the burden that rested on his slave. Often very dependence begat an affectionate interest, and early associations made loving friends without a thought of being equal friends.

"An incident in the life of Bishop Polk, of Louisiana, will illustrate what is asserted. He was by inheritance and through marriage a large slaveholder. He had no scruples of conscience to make him think of freeing his bondmen; but his conscience bade him care for them—for their bodies and for their souls. In fact, a sense of responsibility was one cause of loss of fortune to him. He was their master, and therefore could not escape from duty toward them. As in other respects dutiful, he was their faithful religious teacher.

"One of these slaves, who was his brother in Christ, was drawing nigh to death. The bishop had administered to him as a Christian priest. Still watching by him he said, 'Tom, is there anything else I can do for you?' The answer was, 'Yes, master, if you will only lie down by me on the bed, and put your arm round my neck, and let me put my arm round your neck as we used to do when boys lying under the green walnut trees, I think I could die more easy.' Thus lying in the embrace of his master he passed away."

The average Northerner, on the other hand, while he may without concern see the negro at the ballot-box, occupying a neighboring stall at the theater, or with equal freedom using public conveyances, is nevertheless indifferent to his welfare. With a shrug he leaves him to take his chances with other men, and rather prefers he should keep at a distance. With few exceptions, he is as unlikely as the Southerner to entertain him at his table, and feels very thoroughly that he has too long been a prominent factor in politics—in which he is undoubtedly right, though the blame is not to be laid to the colored man—and so desires to hear as little of him as possible.

This marked difference of feeling toward the colored people has long prevented hearty co-operation of the two sections of the country in working earnestly for their good. Yet until such union there is little hope of their true advancement. As President Haygood* well says, "In no rational view of the case is this a question that one political party or section of the country can solve alone. If both parties, and both parties working together, can solve it, they will do well. It would

* Rev. A. G. Haygood, D.D., President of Emory College, Oxford, Ga., who in " Our Brother in Black," while writing as a Southerner, deals with the problem with great fairness and cleverness.

be a misfortune to the country if either one of the parties could solve it independently of the other party. This is not a party or sectional problem, *it is the task of the nation."*

In this matter of drawing a "color line" in the churches there is little difference in the two sections of the country. In an old New England church, we well remember the long line of neatly dressed people with black faces coming from the far-off gallery to make their communion after those *"in gold rings and goodly apparel"* had first been served at the Lord's Table. This custom is not exceptional in the North.

To expect more of Southerners than of Northerners is unreasonable. It is certainly the duty of clergy and congregations of all Christian churches to welcome colored communicants with that charity which bears in mind that God is "no respecter of persons," but where there are a sufficient number of colored people, it is no doubt, at least while prejudice remains so strong, best for themselves that they should have churches of their own. In the South there would often not be room in existing congregations for colored people. Hiring a seat in "pewed churches" is contrary to their customs and generally beyond their means. They are not unnaturally too sensitive to occupy "free seats" in some obscure corner. But there are other and still more justifiable reasons. Only by gathering them into separate congregations can services and teachings be adapted to their condition and wants, and so only can an active and personal share in parochial work be theirs. As a part of a white congregation, they would remain an inappreciable element. There could then be no sphere of labor for colored clergy. The colored people would not probably be found in choirs, vestries or parochial societies, nor taking part in diocesan affairs. They would therefore have little personal interest in the Church's life and growth.

With these arguments the delegation from S. Philip's urged their request. A place where they could continue a distinct congregation was promised them if Bishop Whittingham approved.

The bishop readily gave his approval, although on account of some former relations to the congregation he requested us to begin our work among colored people without relation to S. Philip's, and under another name. The name of S. Mary the Virgin was adopted for the new enterprise. A few colored women who had long been communicants of Mount Calvary Church and some others gathered from the neighborhood were assembled for the first service on Sunday morning, March 23, 1873, in the chapel of the All Saints Mission House, No. 85 Preston St.

The All Saints Sisters of the Poor, at the request of the Mount Calvary clergy and with the hearty sanction of the Bishop of Maryland, had sent from their mother house in London three of their number to establish the Order in Baltimore. These English Sisters took a lively interest in the colored

people. Until we could obtain a building they
loaned their chapel, and soon after, one of their
number was assigned to work among the colored
people, for whom a Mission House and school on
Biddle Street were opened. At the first service, a
celebration of the Holy Communion, the priest in
charge was celebrant, assisted by the Rev. Evelyn
Bartow.

While worshiping in the Mission House we
had as server a comical little fellow, Henry, the
son of our cook at the Clergy House. He shall
describe himself. The Rev. Arthur Ritchie, during that year one of our number, had observed the
way in which the colored people sort each other
out into " brown skinned men," " dark skinned
men," " yellow men," " light " and " fair " people, while with cruel irony they sometimes speak
of white people in distinction from " colored " as
"*plain* people ! " This accuracy of classification
is apt to puzzle the uninitiated. So Mr. Ritchie
asked the boy, " Henry, are you a dark skinned
boy or a yellow skinned ? " " I'se neither, Massa
Ritchie, I'se kinder ginger snap color, sah ! "

Red cassocks had been suggested for use in the
choir, by Mr. Smith, the bishop's secretary, who
had won the bishop to the plan.

Later, owing to their offending some over-tender
consciences, the bishop said one day, " Perry, you'd
better send those cassocks to the dye-house." The
hint was taken and they became a more sober blue.
On the morning that the red cassock was to delight

Henry, in spite of the anticipation, he, as was not unusual, overslept himself. The cassock, owing to some delay, remained unfinished, even sleeveless, in the sisters' workroom. About the middle of the service the celebrant was startled by a stealthy noise, and turning, saw Henry creeping on all fours toward the altar, his black face, legs, and arms protruding from the unfinished cassock like the black head and legs of a huge red-winged beetle.

Two months later we obtained a small hall on Pennsylvania Avenue, near Orchard Street. Sunday, May 18, we held our first service there. The larger portion of S. Philip's congregation, about thirty communicants, then joined us. Had the present beautiful marble altar and mosaic reredos then adorned Mount Calvary, Mr. Richey could not have referred truthfully—as mentioned in Mr. Mason's letter—to St. Mary's as its equal. But the extemporized chancel was very pretty. The altar was large and effective, its three retables brilliant with lights and flowers. Behind and at the sides were hangings of white and blue. A surpliced choir had been trained by Mrs. Mason, and the singing was such as many a church might have emulated.

By the kindness of a friend, for whose generous aid we cannot be too grateful, we were enabled to call the Rev. Alfred B. Leeson, to assist in the work. He had just entered on his labors when the same friend purchased for our use a neat chapel of white "Baltimore County marble,"

3

situated on Orchard Street near the corner of
Madison Avenue. Orchard Street is exclusively
inhabited by colored people ; St. Mary's Street in
the rear of the chapel hardly less so. Yet both
are broad well-shaded streets, quite different from
the alleys into which most of the colored people
are crowded. The chapel is conveniently situated
almost directly across the street from Mount Calvary Church. On Sunday, S. Matthew's day,
Sept. 21st, of the same year we held our first service in our new home.

So with blessings beyond our fondest hopes, the
work began among a people whom the Church had
so long neglected. To the first effort in their behalf they heartily responded, and from that time
have not failed to do their part. An intimate knowledge of them has deepened the impression that while
they are as far removed from the ideal of the novel-
ist as the genuine Indian is from Cooper's " noble
savage," yet they possess amiable and noble traits
which have received scanty justice from their
white brethren. In estimating the character of
the colored people of this country, it is difficult to
do them justice on account of their juxtaposition
with a people of chiefly English origin. By no
people are they more likely to be severely judged,
in contrast to no people would they appear to
greater disadvantage.

The character of the English speaking people,
what is popularly termed Anglo-Saxon character,
has undoubtedly many noble traits. The English

folk seem fitted and destined to become masters of
a great part of the world. In colonizing, in the
extending their language and in controlling
thought, they rival the Greeks, no less than in extending their empire they rival the Romans. They
carry with them into all lands sturdy virtues,
honesty, truthfulness, energy, and a sort of robust
manliness which never fails to command respect.

But their advent is not an unmixed joy to a
weaker race. They are prone to exterminate as
well as predominate. Before the march of their
superior institutions the aborigines vanish. Unlike the warmer hearted Latin and Celtic races,
the Englishman has little power of adaptation to
the national peculiarities of other nations. Where
he cannot convert to his own standard he tramples
out. What he cannot assimilate he will not tole-
rate. As the genuine Englishman will eat, dress,
and work in a tropical country as he would in
England, and despises all food but joints of beef and
mutton, no matter in what climate, so he finds it
hard to do justice to virtues that he does not possess,
or condone the absence of those that are character-
istically English. He has little power to put himself in another's place. To the true Britisher, one
of another nation, and still more one of another
race, is as the Gentile to the Jew, the barbarian to
the Greek.

An acquaintance of the writer stood in an Italian
post office when an Englishman came in to have a
letter registered. The Italian postmaster, who

could understand though he could not speak English, took the letter and, in Italian, inquired the name. The Englishman, who did not understand a word of Italian, replied somewhat sternly, "I wish it registered." "Si, Si, Signore, certamente; che nome? With reddening face, the Englishman thundered, "I wish it registered." How long these pertinent replies might have followed cannot be known, for the American gentleman at this point stepped forward and said : " The postmaster is quite ready to send the letter, sir, but asks your name." "Aw !" replied the now pacified representative of the British lion, "I did not understand. How unfortunate for these Italians that *they do not understand our language.*"

Exclusive of the negro, the inhabitants of the United States are chiefly of English origin. As Mr. Freeman well observes in his sagacious but thoroughly English " Impressions of the United States," "though the infusion of foreign elements has been large, yet it is the English kernel which has assimilated these foreign elements." It is our privilege, as he claims for us, as it may well be our pride, to belong to the great family of " English folk." Yet this "infusion of foreign element," as well as many other causes, as of climate, national institutions, early French influences and the like, have greatly modified in us the character which we may term English or British, since Anglo-Saxon is not unreasonably condemned in the above work as a misnomer. Not without the loss of some of the sterner, manly characteristics of our English forefathers, the bluntness, the shyness, the exclusiveness, the inadaptability of the genuine Britisher have also to a great extent disappeared in his "American cousin." But we have not lost those English traits which serve to drive out and exterminate, instead of raising and assimilating, weaker races, as may be seen in our attitude toward the three of the great families of mankind in our land—the Indian, the Negro, the Mongolian. The presence of these alien races is an offense to us, largely because they are so dissimilar to ourselves, while their virtues—virtues which those who know them best testify are characteristic in each of these races—count for little because they are not English virtues. For example, do gentleness, endurance, gratitude, warm affection, amiability, a dread of bloodshed, and deep, devotional spirit count for nothing in the negro character? But it is his alleged dishonesty and unchastity that are alone dwelt upon, and chiefly because he is contrasted not with the white man in general, but with English speaking peoples, who especially pride themselves, though we fear with ever lessening claim, on honesty and chastity. But the African is a son of the tropics. His blood has boiled for ages in equatorial heat. Aside from all questions of the influence of slavery, resemblances to his native character among white peoples should be sought not among the descendants of those who were nursed amid the cold mists and bracing blasts of the North Sea, but among the children of warmer climes beneath southern skies. If he is lacking in the ferociousness, the love of slaughter, and the devotion to selfish interests which are ever reappearing in those in whose veins flows the blood of the Norsemen and the Vikings, it is not strange that he should reveal the passionate yet indolent tendencies of all Southern races.

It was during a brief stay in Italy that this thought forcibly impressed the writer. The kindness of dear and honored friends there, whose patience with his inquisitiveness he cannot too gratefully acknowledge, gave him unusual advantage in gaining an insight into the character of the people, in spite of his visit being confined to a few weeks. No one would think, unless from very Anglican prejudice, of classing as among inferior races the inhabitants of that fairest of all lands, the successors and at least in part the descendants of the people who once ruled the world, who in later times have gained more glorious victories in the realm of thought and art, by Dante, by Petrarch and Sappho, by Raphael and Michael Angelo. If to-day young Italy rising to a third career of greatness, with the invincible and immortal vigor which neither Rome's decline, nor Papal oppression could shackle with eternal chains, is not allowed to be, as the writer felt, the most fascinating and in many respects one of the noblest of the peoples of the earth, yet who would dare to look with condescension upon the Roman or the Florentine, or

even the Neapolitan or the Venetian? Yet in the
working classes of these lovely cities, especially of
the last two named, are found many of those traits
which are common, as we believe, to all Southern
natures, but from which as "negro characteristics"
we turn with aversion. An intelligent English lady,
who has for many years kept house near Naples,
spoke of her love for the lower classes of Southern
Italy, but she added that one must know them
well to feel so toward them. The first impression
was of their dishonesty and untruthfulness. Sums
of money and valuables might be left unguarded,
but she knew that many families were being fed
from the pilfering from her store-room. This they
did not consider stealing. They seldom told ma-
licious or deliberate lies, but their excuses did not
bear the light of truth. Winning in their ways,
grateful and faithful to those they loved, they
were a race of affectionate children. Could the
colored servants of a Southern household be more
accurately described?

In loveliest Venice too, the chorus that early in
the morning wakens one who dwells near the
mouth of the Grand Canal, the ceaseless chatter of
gondoliers, peasants and beggars gathered on the
Riva, mingled with snatches of song, mock quarrels
and bursts of laughter, while from the narrow
"Calli" are heard the pathetic, pleading cries of
the hucksters, chanting the merits of their wares,
are not unlike the noises that are heard through
the open windows in Baltimore at the same hour,

when the sprinkling of streets and the washing of marble steps begin. The colored people are not less like the Venetian, as Howell cleverly describes him, " loving best of everything a clamorous quarrel carried on with the canal between him and his antagonist ; but next to this he loves to spend his leisure at the ferry in talking of eating and of money."

Howell quotes a recent Venetian writer as saying, " No one can deny that our populace is loquacious and quick witted, but on the other hand no one can deny that it is regardless of improvement. Venice, a city exceptional in its construction, its customs, and its habits, has also an exceptional populace. It still feels, although sixty-eight years have passed, the influence of the system of the fallen Republic, of that oligarchic government, which affording almost every day some amusement of the people, left them no time to think of their offended rights."

The " cake walk " and nightly dance served much the same purpose in causing the slave to forget his bondage. Even the form of their religion, the wild orgies of the bush-meeting, left their moral training as neglected as the empty ecclesiastical pageants of the Italian Church left that of the Venetians. The lack of work at Venice, and the small amount of work expected or required from the slave also have produced like results. Both people seem, in the expressive language of the colored people, to have " been born tired." So long has every career worthy of ambition been closed to them, they have ceased to strive. Nature adapts herself. The organs of sight in the mole become small, in the fish of subterranean caves they disappear. No wonder the negro has in many respects (as he expresses it), "de-vanced instead of advanced." The great difficulty of stimulating the colored people to throw off this lethargy has been one of the chief discouragements to be met by those who have labored among them. But a trait that has for ages been crushed out demands time for restoration. The convalescent walks with but feeble steps at first in daisied fields, which yet he may have viewed from his window with longing eyes.

The two peoples have the same power of lightly throwing off sorrow and misery and laughing through their tears. They have grown content with their lot. A feast of polenta and a half glass of the cheap native wine, and the Venetian is happy as a king. Its memories furnish an agreeable topic for thought and conversation the rest of the day. It is of little moment if he sleep under his cloudless beautiful sky. Climate makes the colored man of America differ from him in this last respect only. To pay his rent and keep a roof over his head is his first anxiety. Landlords prefer colored tenants to white ; they say that they are more sure of their rent. In the matter of eating there is a closer resemblance to the Italian. None enjoy good eating more than the colored people. They are born cooks and epicures. Soft shell crabs, canvas backs and terrapin are more frequently found at their feasts than would be supposed. But they are as cheerful and content when they return to their frugal meals—if meals they have. Many households have no regular meals. Each member of the family comes in from his work when he can, "snatches a bite"—his mouth as full of laughter as of food—and is off again.

This simple, childlike nature, improvident, cloaking misery beneath laughter, has been at once the protection and the curse of both peoples. One who lives among the Italian peasantry or the Southern freedmen grows to expect little of them, and to love them and indulge them as children. Who can resist the pleading look from the deep violet eyes of the picturesque youth who has listlessly guided your gondola to the landing, when you know that a few soldi dropped into a hand extended with a courtier's grace will bring a gleam of sunshine from the beautiful eyes and from the full ripe Italian lips a torrent of benedictions that will flatter you into thinking yourself generous? If the colored people have not as a rule the same eloquence of beauty, they are not destitute of grace, and it is with much the same feeling that the true Southerner regards the "old time" negro.

There are few street beggars among the colored people. There is little need of soliciting on the street. Besides the fact that they are content with little, and that although they may berate each other with their tongues they are very generous in

aiding each other in real need, there is for the older
generation "ole massa" as a last resort. Aunt
Tilly "Has jis dropped roun' to see if Massa's bin
well all dis time, cause Aunt Tilly thought a mos'
Massa must ha' done gone away, caus' she 'lows
it seems like he mos' forgot Aunt Tilly so long,"
and as the faithful old soul drops a courtesy with
the words, "Spec' Honey ain't goin' to forgit Aunt
Tilly dis time no how, is ye ?" few genuine true-
hearted Southerners would resist the appeal. Much
of this old patriarchal feeling remains in all parts
of the South, and many an old household servant
is kept comfortably housed and fed by children
and even grandchildren of former owners.

There is something which peculiarly appeals to
the strong Anglo-Saxon heart in this relation of
dependence, as the strong-hearted oak seems to
woo the vine to wind its tendrils about its sturdy
limbs.

Yet however kind-hearted this manner of treat-
ing the colored people may be, and perhaps necessary in past relations, it will not now fit him for
that struggle in life which in his changed condition he cannot escape. For the younger generation at least it is mistaken kindness. It belongs
to that same tendency of which Howell complains
in regard to the Venetians, "really fatal to all sincerity of judgment, and incalculably mischievous
to such down-fallen people as have felt the baleful
effects of the world's sentimental, impotent sympathy."

There are graver charges against the colored man which we must not ignore. To his alleged dishonesty we have already alluded. Clear notions of the right of property is probably among all nations a result of civilization. The absolute savage cannot draw a very distinct line between "meum" and "tuum." Slavery was a poor instructor in this principle of social economy, and it is not remarkable that such ideas of the right of possession as the African may have brought from his native wilds should have been sadly confused. Dr. Tucker, in his "Relations of the Church to the Colored Race,"* a witness that cannot be impugned as prejudiced in the negro's favor, thus apologizes for this habit of pilfering. "It never seemed wrong for the slave to steal from his own master. He was but property himself, and it was 'all in the family.' Besides he worked for nothing, and it seemed to him but justice that he should enjoy some of his master's good things, for which his labor paid. Something of this feeling the owners also had, so that petty pilfering was looked upon by both races as a matter of course, a thing to be winked at. * * * This was always in all countries one of the natural results of slav-

---

* We by no means agree with much in Dr. Tucker's pamphlet, but we respect his candor, and as a discussion of the question from a strongly Southern stand-point, it demands an attentive consideration. Both it and the able answer by Dr. Crummel, a representative negro, should be carefully read by those who would master the "negro problem."

ery. * * * They would rarely steal money even when they had opportunity."

This amounts to an acquittal of the negro as a race of any characteristic tendency to steal. To help himself to his master's goods is the natural instinct of the slave of any race. It was so of the Roman slaves, who were captives of all races. The slave's way of looking at the question is well illustrated by Sambo, who, when rebuked for stealing his master's turkey, replied, "Sambo no steal turkey. Sambo massa's, and turkey massa's. Turkey jis much massa's when he inside Sambo as ober."

Were dishonesty universal among the colored people as a result of past slavery, it could not be a cause of surprise. But it is not. There are men and women among the colored people upon whose honesty entire trust may be placed. We may well hope, therefore, that in a state of freedom, and with the restraints with which civilized society protects itself, the negro will become sufficiently honest to cause the white man to look to his own record on Wall Street before he points the finger at his black brother. As to the charge of universal untruthfulness in the negro, Dr. Tucker points out that the "instinct of concealment" also is a necessary result of slavery. It is indeed the exceptional school-boy who will not lie out of a flogging. Such virtue could not be expected in the slave. It may be predicted, however, that the negro, in common with all Oriental peoples, and with Southern Europeans, will never have as strict a standard of veracity as that which seems to be naturally connected with the bluntness and coldness of Northern races.

But the gravest charge that has been made against the negro, one that may not be ignored in any candid consideration of his character, is, that chastity is unknown to him. It must be acknowledged that revolting facts seem to justify the assertion. Atrocious deeds that appear not infrequently in our papers seem to make men guard their wives and daughters from some of their former slaves as from brute beasts.

It has been customary to assert that licentiousness is an element of the African character brought with him from his native home, a necessary trait of barbarous life. The assertion seems wholly unwarranted. It is apparently only a welcome but futile subterfuge of the white man, who may well shrink from regarding the degradation of his black brother as the result of his own institution.

Dr. Crummell, who has lived twenty years in West Africa, says of the native women, "Their maidenly virtue, the instinct to chastity, is a marvel. I have no hesitation in the generalization that in West Africa, every female is a virgin to the day of her marriage. The harlot class is unknown in all their tribes. I venture the assertion that any one walking through Pall Mall, London, or Broadway, New York, for a week would see more indecency in look and act than he could discover in an African town in a dozen years.

During my residence there I only *once* saw an indecent act." Bishop Penick, formerly of Cape Palmas, himself a Southerner, and "called into court" as a witness by Dr. Tucker, says, "It is a very rare exception to find a young woman or man by look or gesture conveying an immodest impression. So one may walk through a heathen town full of almost naked people and see less immodesty than in some of our most fashionable streets in some of our best cities." "It is a very rare thing to see a native man or woman do an immodest act or to say an immodest word."

In order to add testimony wholly independent of any controversial bias, the following letter has been obtained from a distinguished missionary of the University Mission to Central Africa. It is due to the kindness of a friend, Mr. Edward Winkley—himself preparing at the Missionary Theological College at Dorchester, for the same mission field—who asked Mr. Johnson's opinion of the statement contained in Dr. Tucker's speech, "That what we call morality, whether in the relation of the sexes, or in the sense of truthfulness, or in the sense of honesty, has no lodgment whatever in the native African heart." This is his reply:

Jan. 23, 1884.

DEAR SIR,

Mr. W. has brought under my notice some paragraphs which represent the negro as devoid of moral feeling. After seven years intimate communion with Africans iu East Africa between 5° south and 16° south, I feel called on to testify to the moral practice of the natives I have come across.

The marriage tie is respected, and the youth of each village lead a life generally free from gross immorality. Partly owing to the hardships attaching to their life, they are very slaves to eating and drinking, and even if native beer abounds are very besotted. Any use of bad language is a gross offense against society and is only picked up from the coast people. Venereal diseases are only known as imported from the coast. Lying is stigmatized as from a bad heart, and in judging of apparent acts of deception we must remember that very often a different standard of truth is adopted in dealing with foreigners, even when people are honest in dealing among themselves. Theft is summarily punished, and we often leave articles about in reach of natives and nothing is lost. The difference between a good and a bad heart is considered a radical one, and all good actions are no mere chance phenomena but due to the good heart, and *vice versa*. Here we see the terrible results of the slave trade. When the people reach the coast they have had a shock sufficient to banish ideas of decency, of fidelity, and of all self-respect, and may well doubt if the good heart exists, and cease to seek it. No wonder if slaves are grossly sensual and sometimes thieves, and lie to them they have no respect for. (Signed)

W. P. JOHNSON.

An All Saints' Sister, now in Baltimore, but who has been laboring for five years in quite another part of Africa, at the Cape, permits me to add that what is stated above of the natives of Central Africa, is quite true, not only of the Bushmen and Hottentots, but also of the many negroes at the Cape, brought originally as slaves from the interior, and that the colonists much prefer the

latter as servants to such whites as they are likely
to obtain, on account of superior honesty and
truthfulness.

From the testimony of such competent witnesses
we must conclude either that the African tribes
are exceptionally chaste, or what, alas! seems but too
probable, that unchastity being not a law, but a
violation of nature, is a result of civilization and a
lesson which the white man has taught the negro.

Can it be questioned that this lesson has been
taught in the most degrading way during the two
hundred years of slavery? Dr. Crummell draws
the picture in very plain language and with a
vehemence which is natural to an indignant cham-
pion of the negro race.

After allowing that there was a large class of
good slaveholders who, "like baronial lords, like
patriarchs of old, like the grand aristocrats of
civilized society, were kind, generous, humane "—
they were "noblemen "—he proceeds to describe
those who were of a far different character:

"They herded their slaves together like animals.
They were allowed to breed like cattle. The marriage relation was utterly disregarded. All through
the rural districts, on numerous plantations, the
slaves for generations merely mated as beasts.
They were separated at convenience, caprice, or at
the call of interest. When separated each took up
with other men or women as lust or inclination
prompted. Masters and ministers of the gospel
taught their slaves not only that there was no sin

in such alliances, but that it was their duty to make new alliances. . . . . The cases are numerous where men, sold from one plantation to another, have had six or eight living wives, and women as many living husbands. Nay, more than this, I have the testimony where one man less than fifty years old was the father of over sixty children ; of another man who was kept on a plantation with full license as a mere breeder of human beings ! . . . . But it should be remembered that these gross sins are common as well among the whites of the South as among its black population. It filled *them* full of lust as well as their victims."

Revolting as this description may be, we are not aware that these, and even more distressing details, are anywhere denied. Dr. Tucker, in his own pamphlet, admits, indeed emphasizes, these same facts. Every one who has worked among the freedmen is perfectly familiar with this condition of things. In our own work we have had under our pastoral care women who, in former days, were kept upon plantations solely for the purpose of raising children for sale from fathers, both white and colored, selected for their valuable qualities. Even in the case of good owners, it was, on large plantations, the household servants who chiefly experienced their kindness or profited by their example. The management of the field hands was necessarily left to subordinates, and their great numbers prevented their being housed or treated like human beings. Many Southerners sought to excuse to themselves this system by believing they were not human beings. Learned professors wrote books, still extant, excluding them from the plan of redemption, and a lady of a large Southern city told the writer she had become unpopular among her friends for expressing a belief that they had souls. The example of the whites with whom their intercourse was most intimate did nothing to lift them from their sins. From unimpeachable testimony the writer knows of bands of dissolute young men who, taking advantage of the strict regulations which forbade, under penalty of severe punishment, the free colored people from being out of their houses after 10 P.M., or from social gatherings, without expensive permits, would drag men from their homes, beat and bind them, and return to outrage their wives and daughters. As a colored man's testimony was not received in the courts, there was no redress.

Says Dr. Tucker : "That the white people were at heart no better than themselves, they were positive. Had they not proof? Whence came so many mulattoes?" The temptation which came from the opportunity of being the petted favorite of an owner and escaping hardship as the price of virtue, especially as the tempter who asked consent had the right to compel, was still more demoralizing than acts of violence.

So by the force of example, by the dictates of self-interest, and often by compulsion, the colored people, whether slaves or free, were taught to disregard every principle of purity. How can chastity be looked for in less than twenty years after emancipation, when for two hundred years they had been trained to disregard it ?

With such a training it were not strange if chastity *were* utterly unprized or even unknown among a people who are all either freedmen or the descendants of slaves. But such is not the case. In spite of past traditions, in spite of their defective religious systems, and notwithstanding the prevalent licentiousness and increasing tendency to disregard the sanctity and indissolubility of marriage among Americans, to whom they should look for a better example, a great number of former slaves since emancipation have settled down into chaste and orderly households.

If in parts of the South there are, as is claimed, great numbers living together without legal marriage, so there are other parts where so to live excludes the guilty from all intercourse with the more orderly and intelligent. It must be admitted, indeed, that the great mass of colored people are far, very far from prizing chastity as they should, yet there are many young women in our own congregation whom we not only could point out as virtuous, but some as modest and as pure in thought and feeling as could be wished. To reach this point when surrounded by temptations unknown to those in higher circles of society, is surely a proof of what grace can do for them,

and should be a sufficient incentive to hasten with
Christian love to bring others to the same condition.

We recall these things of the past not to revive
old issues. The institution of slavery has forever
passed away, as much to the satisfaction of all the
better class of Southern people as of Northern.
The former may condemn the manner of emancipation, and some of its results; few, if any, regret
that slavery is no more. Let it be forgotten and
forgiven, a curse upon the master no less than upon
the slave; a curse, which if it found its stronghold
in the South, was at first chiefly brought upon the
land by the North. But in judging of the present
character of the colored people, or in forecasting
their future, these facts of the past cannot be
ignored without leading to injustice and error.
If, too, the white man is chiefly responsible for
these evils, it should lead him to pity rather than
censure, to hasten to remedy the evil they have
caused rather than shrink from its results. What
selfishness and lust have wrought, that the grace of
God can in His own good time counteract. If it
lead any to more earnest efforts to hasten this
time, the purpose of the writer will be attained.

It has been hoped, moreover, that the foregoing
consideration of the traits of the negro, as a race,
and the comparison of him with other types of
mankind, might somewhat indicate the character
of the laborer who will most successfully work for
his good and the spirit in which the work must
be undertaken.

There have been strong advocates of late for increasing, at any price, the number of colored clergy, and many have affirmed that they only can effectually accomplish the conversion of their people. The necessity of colored clergy and laymen has been strongly pressed by a recent conference of colored clergy of our Church held in New York. Any suggestions that come from the most intelligent of their own race, should be heartily welcomed by those who are truly interested in them, and demand respectful consideration. The objection that is said to have been made by a bishop to such a meeting, that the Church knew well enough how to conduct her work and needed no suggestions, is absurd. The proof of its absurdity is the lamentable failure of the Church thus far in the work. Yet we regret the apparent meaning of the resolutions that none but colored clergy should work among colored people; a meaning which we have been informed upon the best authority it was not intended they should convey. In the main they are right. Clergy of their own race can accomplish a work among them that no white man can do, however willing to make all requisite sacrifices. They alone can enter into the very heart's sanctuary of the negro and view things from his standpoint. They are free from suspicions with which a great number of the colored people continue to view the most devoted of their white friends.

But the clergy of their own race must come

from the very best and most favored of their
people, and be fully equipped to bear favorable
comparison with their white brethren. No inferior article will pass. An unfortunate but
general disposition to disparage those of their
own race makes it difficult under the most favorable circumstances for colored clergy to gain the
respect of their people. If the colored clergy are
treated as inferiors by their white brethren, or if
there be any recognized difference of intellectual
requirements, or any ecclesiastical disabilities by
which they are distinguished from them, their
failure is certain.

No doubt the permanent diaconate after the
primitive model might be usefully revived irre-
spective of color. It might be a distinct Order
with a confessedly lower grade of scholarship.
Catechists, teachers, and lay-readers may all be
useful among the colored people, as they may
among any people. But any " class legislation "
lowering the standard of the priesthood on the
" color line " will certainly prove fatal to the
Church's growth among them.

Such legislation is, moreover, wholly unnecessary. There are many intelligent, sensible, well-
mannered young colored men who would require
no dispensation from literary qualifications. They
need only to be sought out by the Church, assured
of support and of brotherly sympathy, and properly
trained and educated. Their education will take
time. Better hasten slowly than repent at leisure.

In the mean time white clergy must do much of the work. For many reasons it is best they should be engaged in the work for many years to come, even if there were as many well educated colored clergy as could be wished. There are traits of character and results of civilization which can thus best be imparted from the dominant to the advancing race. Thus too, will the bond of fellowship be best maintained between the two races and mutual suspicions allayed.

White clergy, to be of any use among them, must be liberal minded, large hearted, sympathetic men. They must not regard them solely from an Anglican standpoint, and not be blind to their virtues and amiable traits. They must be ready to become as a negro to the negroes if they would win the negro, as fully as St. Paul became as a Jew to the Jews or as a Gentile to the Gentiles. They must be moved as little by bitter taunt and prejudice as was our Lord by the words "This man receiveth sinners and eateth with them." The missionary does not hesitate to live on most familiar terms with Chinese, Hottentot, or Esquimaux. The explorer for mere scientific purposes will do the same. The true friend of the spread of the gospel will learn to dissociate such intercourse from that which is for merely political demagogical purposes. The writer does not blush to own that he has laughed in their joys and wept in their sorrows, eaten with them, slept with them, been their guest and entertained them, known them as dear friends and com-

panions. He who is their spiritual father, and
fears in so doing "to lose his social position," has
no "social position" worth guarding. Yet the
writer does not deny that in the earlier years of
his work he sometimes winced under taunt and
scorn, and that he keenly felt some dear friends'
dislike to be seen with one who had been on the
street in the company of his colored parishioners. A
wounded soldier may tear the poisoned barb from
the quivering flesh lest it impede him in battle, but
it is not without anguish. But it is to be acknowledged with devout gratitude to God that in the
last ten years a marked change in sentiment has
taken place. Some who once looked with suspicion
on the work now fearlessly aid and defend it.
Some of the most ardent Southerners championed
it from the start. Notably did one of Maryland's
noblest laymen, now called to rest, who languished
in a Northern fortress for his principles during the
war, but never wavered in his confidence in the
clergy who directed the work at S. Mary's, nor
failed in finding an excuse for their mistakes.

It is likely that clergy who will be ready to go
forth in this spirit to labor among the colored people will be largely drawn from the higher ranks of
society. Such men, it is said, show most endurance
in military life—they are certainly not least likely
to "endure hardness as good soldiers of JESUS
CHRIST." They are also least sensitive about "en-
dangering their social position." It is at all events
absolutely necessary that they should have acquired

refinement and the marks of good breeding, if not "to the manner born." Few so quickly detect the gentleman as the Southern negro. They respect "quality," but "have no use fur po' white trash." Persons of refinement can most freely mingle with them without losing their respect, or without exhibiting the condescension which they resent. At an after-dinner speech at an anniversary of that admirable institution, the Missionary Theological College at Dorchester, England, a gentleman of long experience in Central Africa spoke of this same instinctive recognition of a gentleman as a trait of the natives, who in their own language distinguished between "gentlemen" and "gentlemen gentlemen." "There is doubtless," he said, "work for all in the ministry, but send only the sons of gentlemen to Africa."

It was the need of men of refinement and intelligence who would go forth in the spirit we have indicated that was felt by that noble martyr of our communion, Bishop Patterson, in his work among a kindred race, the blacks of the Melanesian Isles.

"It was never the way," says his admirable biographer, "where Mr. Patterson reigned, to have one sort of work for the white and another for the black. Black people are no worse than white, and it was contrary to the main idea of the mission that a white man, because he was white, should have a right to make a black man work because he was black." "In truth, what he *did* want, were men equal to himself, and he was the only man who did not know that such men are rare. He would not have any one who would despise the natives, and wish to make Englishmen of them. God did not make all the world English, and what these natives were intended to be was a something very different from Englishmen. They must lead a godly and a Christian life, but he wished to teach them to do this by making them see for themselves what was wrong in their own customs, and leave it off for that reason, not merely copy what their teachers did."

These principles, upon which the Church in the South Sea Islands was successfully built, are those upon which rest the conversion of the colored people of the United States.

CHAPTER III.

THE property which was placed at the disposal
of the clergy of Mount Calvary Church was an
edifice built for the use of a small congregation
of Swedenborgians. It was of white Baltimore
limestone (an inferior kind of marble, easily
worked, and effective in appearance). The building was two stories, the lower, with floor a little below the street line, had been used as a boys' school-
room, the upper as a room for services and worship.
It was about fifty feet long and forty feet broad,
outside measurements. Soon after we had begun
to use it, a porch was added in front, in which was
placed a double staircase leading to the upper floor.
The design of this addition, while in keeping with
the rest of the building, relieved the front on
Orchard Street. By it, very considerable addition
was made to the seating capacity of the chapel.

In 1878, it was found that the work required an
enlargement of the building. The generous giver
of the chapel assured the clergy that the houses
and land in the rear, fronting fifty-five feet on S.
Mary's Street, would be given whenever the time
came that an addition could be made without incurring debt. To this end, by the help of those

CHAPEL OF ST.MARY THE VIRGIN

interested in this work, and in answer to personal
appeals among the clergy of the church about ten
thousand dollars was raised by the priest in charge
of the work.   The property was conveyed to the
Diocese of Maryland in trust.   The dwellings on
S. Mary's Street were removed, and on Sunday,
September 7, 1879, the corner stone of the addition was laid by the Rev. Dr. Rich, Dean of the
Convocation of Baltimore, in the presence of a large
congregation of clergy and people.   The addition
was about seventy feet long by fifty-five feet wide,
and is so constructed that it furnishes transepts
and chancel, while the older portion is the nave of
a church about one hundred and thirty feet long.
By the side of the chancel is a porch with stairs
leading to S. Mary's Street, a choir room, about
sixteen feet square, an organ room and priests'
vesting room.   The architectural treatment of the
old portion made it possible for the accomplished
and attentive architects, Messrs. Wyatt & Sperry,
to make the new part, while agreeing with that to
which they were adding in general design, in detail
much more impressive, and, while not carrying
the new walls to any greater height than the old,
by breaking the roof at the transepts, they prevented
the long low look which must otherwise have been,
but which now appears of such liberal proportions
as almost to make the observer forget what the
real size is.   The chancel is about twenty-five feet
wide by twenty-eight deep.   The need of a passage
from one side to the other, behind the altar, made

it necessary to put up a partition which is continued as a screen in front of the east window, and serves as a reredos. The light coming out from either side at times presents a halo-like appearance, a fit accompaniment of the Presence on the altar below.

The chancel arch of brick, supported on two polished Aberdeen granite columns, was erected by the Sunday School, and by friends of the Rev. Harrison H. Webb, the second colored clergyman in Baltimore, as a memorial of him, and of the Rev. Joseph Richey, Rector of Mount Calvary Church at the time that the clergy there undertook this work.

The choir rails of solid oak break on one side into a rounding pulpit. These were the gift of two ladies in memory of a faithful nurse, whose loving care in their childhood is thus recalled. The choir stalls were given by the members of the choir and by the guild. The floor of the choir was laid in wood by the members of the Sinking Fund Association. The altar-rail was the gift of two officers of the army stationed at the fort, who took great interest in S. Mary's. The altar, which had been built by the priest in charge, assisted by the young men of the congregation, does service until a permanent one is provided to take its place.

The work went on with the usual interruptions. No secure foundation for tower and chancel could be found until a depth of sixteen feet had been reached. Other hinderances occurred, and it was not until the Feast of the Purification of the B. V. M., Feb. 2d, 1880, that the services were first held in the new part, and then the walls were but freshly covered with undried mortar, and it was with danger to health that any could sit in the new part of the church. Still no ill effects followed, and from that day on it has been shown that the church was none too large for the people who ought to be gathered in.

The finishing of the church was left until all the cost of the erection of the new part was paid. As this is gradually in process of accomplishment, at divers times steps have been taken for needed articles. The last was the seating of the church with permanent benches, the offerings of individuals and families.

So far God has blessed us. There is much yet to be done. The basement, the front of which is the Vinton Chantry, used for most of the services except those of Sunday, is still unfinished, although used as a school by the sisters. And mortar and paint are called for to make more comfortable and to keep in repair that already erected. We may not be in debt, and we must go on.

The above description of the building is kindly contributed by Mr. Paine, whose indefatigable attention in superintending the building of the addition has made him more familiar than the priest in charge with the dimensions and other architectural details of the building.

The description would suffice were there not in

the chancel some articles of no great intrinsic
value but prized for their quaintness and their associations. Their enumeration will be pardoned by
the casual reader for the sake of those who are more
personally interested. On the altar shelves, or retables, are the cross given by Dr. Mahan, and six
candlesticks engraved with the names of those in
whose memory they were given, Rev. O. P. Vinton,
James D. W. Perry, and H. B. J. On festivals,
vases of flowers and branched candelabra are
added. The panels of the altar are decorated with
curious paintings of the Crucifixion, the Annun-
ciation and the Magi. The latter are oddly enough
represented upon horses. The panels were painted
for the altar by Monks of the Eastern Church in
Jerusalem. They are in the peculiar Oriental
style, brilliant in gold and with stiff conventional
figures. They were the gift of Mr. David Jamal,
a brother of the Rev. Chalcel Jamal, a Syrian priest
of the English Church. Mr. Jamal visited the
clergy in Baltimore, and made an interesting address at S. Mary's. The "Yankee curiosity" dis-
played during his visit is probably remembered by
Mr. Jamal, and will certainly not be soon forgotten
by his traveling companion on a trip made during
his visit to Mount Vernon. Dressed in his native
costume, Mr. Jamal had not only the usual escort
of "ragamuffins" in the streets and circle of in-
quisitors on the steamer, but the climax was
reached on the grounds. Left a moment alone
before the door of the dining hall while his com-

panion secured seats, he was found opposite to an
"American," such as is seen represented on the
stage and portrayed in the pages of English novels,
but the only living specimen we ever remember to
have met. He was a true "Brother Jonathan" of
the Western type, with striped vest and baggy,
short-legged pantaloons. An enormous straw hat
shaded his brown face and shaggy brows. He held
a huge stick extending backward under one arm,
while the end in front of him he energetically
whittled with a jack-knife that might have served
a butcher. As he rolled a "cud" about in his ca-
pacious cheek with a movement of jaws like a con-
templative cow, his calm gaze was steadfastly fixed
on the amazed Syrian. As we approached, the
spell was broken, the huge lips parted, and delib-
erately out rolled the words, "Stranger, *be* you
Injun?" We confess it was with relief we took
the return steamer, but our woes were not ended.
Among the crowd who again gathered around our
friend, one was suddenly struck by a "happy
thought." From the depths of his pocket he produced autograph book and pencil. It was the signal for a hundred hands to dive into as many pock-
ets. In a moment we grasped the situation. Our
turn had come to be the Yankee. We rose, hat in
hand. "Ladies and gentlemen, this Syrian gentleman is my guest and friend. He is not on exhibition, yet all day he patiently and with a gentlemanly forbearance which puts us to shame has
satisfied curiosity. Now you are about to tax him

5

further by asking for innumerable autographs in Syriac. I know he is incapable of refusing you. To-morrow night he addresses my colored congregation, and we take up a collection for his brother, a Christian missionary in Jerusalem. I hope no one will ask for his autograph who does not, as he approaches, drop a quarter in my hat to be added to that offertory." The experiment was not as great a damper on autograph hunting as we had expected, but it added about $8.00 to the offertory. In spite of American curiosity, Mr. Jamal expressed much pleasure in his visit, and on his return sent us these illuminated panels.

The marble altar steps bear the inscription :

† Ecce Agnus stabat supra montem. †

† Agnus Dei, qui tollis peccata mundi, miserere nobis. †

† In Memoriam Rebeccae Webb † Requiescat in Pace. †

Mrs. Webb, the wife of the Rev. Harrison Webb, was one of the most earnest of the communicants who came from S. Philip's to S. Mary's. She lived many years in the family of the lady who gave us our church property, and her faithfulness increased her mistress' interest in her people. The only other objects to be specially noted in the sanctuary, are two stools skillfully and tastefully carved from solid blocks of wood. They are the work of native Africans of the Gold Coast. Seen with several similar specimens at the Centennial Exhibition of

1876 in the English Colonial exhibit, they were supposed to be for sale. On inquiring, it was found that they were to be sent to the Kensington Museum, but the Colonel in Her Majesty's service, who was one of the British commissioners, with great courtesy and kindly interest in the work, promised to do all he could to secure a pair for S. Mary's.

Some months after the close of the exhibition they arrived from England with impressive documents of presentation, officially signed and sealed. To the delight of S. Mary's congregation the daily papers announced that Queen Victoria had presented Acolyte seats to the chapel. It is hoped that the publishing of this will not cause Her Majesty any inconvenience from the "Church Association."

On the oaken choir rail, a legend is carved referring to all to whom memorials are placed in the sanctuary : "Grant unto them, O Lord, Eternal Rest, and let Light Perpetual shine upon them." At the ends of this rail are the polished stone columns which support the chancel arch.

On the sandstone base of one of these memorial columns is the inscription : † In memory of Joseph Richey, Priest. † Him that overcometh will I make a Pillar in the Temple of my God.

On the column on the other side are the words : † In Memory of Harrison H. Webb, Priest. † Be thou faithful unto death, and I will give thee a crown of Life. †

Mr. Richey is already known to the reader. Mr. Webb was for many years the Rector of

S. James' Church, Baltimore. When old age had withdrawn him from active labor he became a devoted attendant of the services of S. Mary's. He often assisted in the service, and occasionally preached. He was buried from S. Mary's.

As the oldest of our male communicants, to whom reference has been made in a previous chapter, stood admiringly before this really fine arch and its two solid pillars, he exclaimed: " Little did I ever expect to see two beautiful columns rising, one in honor of a white priest, the other of a black priest, joined in an arch, symbolizing unity, and pointing toward Heaven." In front of the choir rail is a lectern of oak, its design an eagle standing on an Egyptian column. It bears above the capital of the column the inscription : † In Memory of Oliver Perry Vinton, Priest, † and on the face of the pyramidal base, † Some time Priest of this Church. Entered into Rest June XV, MDCCCLXXX. Whose soul GOD rest and grant a joyful rising in CHRIST JESUS. Amen. The lectern was the gift of Mr. Vinton's brother, Arthur Dudley Vinton, Esq. Upon the lectern is a handsome Bible, one of many gifts to S. Mary's of the Rev. H. G. Batterson, D.D.

Seven lamps hang in the chancel arch. The large central one was the gift of an ever generous friend, Mr. Lyman Klapp ; three were given by S. Clement's, Philadelphia, and the remaining two, recently added, were left as a legacy—in addition to $50 for the Home—by a devoted communicant of

S. Mary's who has lately been laid to rest, Miss Rosa Sythe. Her sister Lizzie, a no less lovely character, dying the year before, left a similar legacy, $50 for the Home, and $50 with which the chapel was provided with a silver chalice.

The basement is divided into three rooms by glass folding doors. The two parts under the nave and transept are used for the day schools and Sunday schools, as well as for evening entertainments, guild and society meetings, and the like. In one of these rooms is the Sunday-school library, in a neat black walnut case, the gift of Mr. Robert Garrett.

The portion of the basement under the chancel is the Vinton Memorial Chantry. Here week-day services are held, thus saving much expense in light and fuel. The Chantry is quite unfinished except the altar and its baldachino. During the completion of the altar, the Rev. II. B. Smythe, who had aided in designing it, went to his father's home in Michigan for a few weeks' vacation. A few days later came tidings of his death. His name was therefore, in loving memory, inscribed on the base of the altar.

The decorated canopy above, resting on Egyptian columns, bears the inscription :

† This Chantry is dedicated to the Glory of God, and in Memory of Oliver Perry Vinton, Priest, by S. Mary's Congregation and Sunday-School, †

and on the space below follows a prayer adapted

from the "Gebetbuch" of the Christian Catholic Church of Switzerland, as given in the General Convention Journal of 1880.

Look, O Lord, upon Thy Son Whom we present before Thee, our pure, holy, and immaculate Sacrifice: For His faithfulness' sake grant unto him and unto all who sleep in Christ a Place of Refreshment, of Life and of Peace.

The Lectern in the Chantry is a portion of the reading-desk of the old S. Paul's Church, afterward used at S. Philip's. On it is the family Bible of Gen. Ambrose E. Burnside, a dear friend of the priest in charge and a generous supporter of his work at S. Mary's. The book was the gift of Mr. W. T. C. Wardwell, a fellow townsman of both the general and the writer.

This completes the list of memorials in the building, excepting three stained glass windows in the church. One contains a suitable inscription to Sister Harriet of All Saints, the Sister Superior when the colored sisterhood was inaugurated. It was a well-deserved tribute of affection from the congregation. Another window is a pretty memorial to two infant children of a lady friend of the work. The third is in memory of Mrs. C. M. C. Mason. The harp in one of the panels recalls her services to S. Mary's, and the scene of the conversion of the Ethiopian by S. Philip her connection with the earlier mission. Another window is about to be added in memory of Sister Mary Clement, and a fourth to Emma Piper, the daughter of one of the Business Committee, a gentle and devout child, who looked forward to being a Sister.

The seats which have been mentioned as the last addition to the church, are "free and unappropriated"—a condition of holding the property. Connected with the free sittings of the two churches, Mount Calvary and S. Mary's, is a little episode of our work worthy of record. It was once the custom for the few colored communicants of the former church to sit in two or three of the rear pews. After Mr. Richey's invitation to the colored people to freely attend the services, and before S. Mary's was provided for them, a considerable number of colored people came, and ignorant of any regulation on the subject, sat wherever there chanced to be a vacant seat. A collision with some of the white congregation followed. The fact was brought to the notice of the clergy. On each pew of Mount Calvary a printed notice declared the seats "free *to all*." The clergy called a Vestry meeting. Nowhere could have been gathered a group more thoroughly representative of Southern sentiment. In the honest and manly tone peculiar to him, Mr. Richey told the Vestry that as the clergy did not wish to remain to the detriment of the parish, they offered their resignations; that if they were to remain they could not consent to there "being a lie on every pew." If the colored people were excluded from free sittings it should be distinctly stated. He reminded them that as he was and ever had been in thorough sympathy with the South, this to him was not a question of politics.

Probably never before in Maryland had the question been directly confronted. For a moment there was silence, which at length was broken by one of the deservedly most influential and honored among the Vestry. He referred to the attachment to the Southern cause of his uncle, who was long imprisoned in Fortress Monroe. Yet that uncle, he said, who was a Roman Catholic, would never accept the privilege granted his age and station of making his confession at the priest's house, for to kneel in the line before the confessional with colored people or the poorest beggars he considered a part of his Catholic practice. "Often," added the nephew, "I have felt inclined to wait to commune at Mount Calvary with the colored people as a proof of my own disapproval of any distinction in God's house." Meanwhile another equally influential member of the Vestry—a distinguished member of the Maryland bar—sat thoughtfully pulling his black mustache. Looking up suddenly, with the serious earnestness that often flashes from his dark eye, he exclaimed, "Gentlemen, let our religion be before our politics; for one I vote that no distinction be made in the seating of the church." Without a dissenting voice the principle was established; their strong and Catholic convictions prevailed.

No serious trouble resulted from the decision. The little irritation shown on the part of some came chiefly from those who had not been identified with the Southern cause. Since S. Mary's has opened, the colored people have preferred to attend services in their own chapel, but when on special occasions, or at celebrations of the Holy Communion at hours that make it more convenient, a few are present at the services of the parish church, there is seldom, we believe, cause to complain of their reception. Bishop Whittingham had, indeed, only consented to the establishment of S. Mary's on the understanding that the colored people were a part of Mount Calvary congregation, worshiping separately only for convenience sake. For this reason, he requested we should have a daily celebration only at Mount Calvary, as it could serve for both. He also suggested, on the same ground, such shortened services at S. Mary's as would be best adapted to the congregation, since the full services were said daily in the parish at Mount Calvary.

Then followed the more amusing side of the story. Mr. Richey had cautioned the white people against crowding out the colored people at the opening services of S. Mary's. The same veteran colored communicant, to whom we have more than once referred, came to the priest in charge seriously troubled because he had heard that white people were to be discriminated against at S. Mary's. He expected to bring with him to the first service a white friend with whom he wished the privilege of sitting, and he hoped in S. Mary's "there would be

no discrimination as to color." This was told with
great glee to the Mount Calvary Vestry, and yet
subsequent events proved the old man's fears not
wholly groundless, for it was often amusing in the
first days of S. Mary's to be summoned just before
vesting for the service, by some lady who had rolled
up to the door in her carriage, and wished to be
told where the white people were to sit. The information that, like the colored people, they were at
perfect liberty to occupy any vacant seat, did not
always seem to be received as a privilege. White
people have shown annoyance when colored people,
in their own chapel, have taken seats next them,
and taking no pains to conceal their displeasure,
have changed their seats. This, however, is exceptional. Many white people come freely to the services, and show a hearty, fraternal sympathy.
Some white people attend and commune at S.
Mary's altogether. It must be confessed, however,
that at night services, when the largest number of
white people, and often wealthy ones, have been
present—it has been observed the offertories are
smallest.

Among the conditions upon which the property
was given was the requirement that the church
should be maintained exclusively by voluntary offerings, without the aid of fairs or festivals of any
kind. No debt was to be incurred, and daily services were to be maintained. These conditions have
been conscientiously kept. About ninety dollars a
month is received through the offertory for current

expenses. Including special collections for missionary and other purposes, the offertory averages annually about one thousand three hundred dollars. The priest in charge receives only his salary as Associate Rector from Mount Calvary Church, but S. Mary's congregation contributes four hundred dollars of the salary of the assistant. As the best means of educating the people to systematic giving, a modified form of the envelope system is adopted. Each attendant of the services is asked to give monthly a specified sum, to be placed in the alms basins in which a collection is made at each Sunday service. The amount of the pledge is left to their own conscience, but the pledge once made they are held strictly accountable for its payment. The financial affairs are conducted by a business committee, nominated on Easter Monday by a ballot of the people, and appointed by the priest in charge. There are two wardens, a treasurer and secretary, and six other members. The most onerous duties fall to the secretary, who keeps the record of the receipts through the envelopes. The other members of the committee distribute the envelopes to the contributors in the districts severally assigned to their care. S. Mary's has been peculiarly fortunate in a succession of faithful officers. Mr. W. H. Bishop, Sen., from the beginning of the work, has combined with the office of warden the responsible duty of treasurer, often to his own cost, but always to the advantage of the church. The office of junior warden has been filled faithfully by

Mr. Richard Mason, Sen., Mr. W. H. Thompson, and now by Mr. Jas. Hughes. Mr. C. M. C. Mason was succeeded as secretary by Mr. W. H. Clarence, a young man of unusual energy and faithfulness in the discharge of duty. Since his enlistment in the army, the post has been filled by Mr. Alfred C. Price, who has industriously carried on the work of his predecessors. The other members at present are, W. H. Thompson, Richard Piper, James Blay, C. A. Johnson, James Royer, H. B. Jackson, Lloyd Toomey.

As has been intimated, the services on Sundays and great festivals are in the church upstairs, those on ordinary week days, the daily evening prayer, a choral service and address on Friday nights, and such early celebrations of the Holy Communion as have been arranged for the week, are in the chantry.

The Holy Communion is celebrated not only each Sunday, but also Thursdays, special holy-days, and in Lent and Advent daily. The usual hour of the celebration is 6:30 A.M. It is so early in order to accommodate many who live at service. When the number of clergy in priests' orders permits, there is a second celebration on Sunday morning at 7:30 A.M. But even when there is only the very early one, a considerable number of men who, employed as barbers or public waiters, have been unable to go to bed on Saturday until long after midnight, yet find their way to the church at this early hour by the cold moonlight of a frosty winter morning. In spite of many being so situated that they can

get out but one or two Sundays during the month,
the average number of communicants on Sunday
mornings during the past year has been 49, the
numbers running from 23 to 90.   This is exclusive
of Christmas and Easter, when there are from 150
to 200.*   In 1873 there were about 30 communicants, there are now 384.   There have been 880
baptisms; 423 persons have received confirmation.
Many of these have sought employment in other
cities, and so the seed is scattered.   This is one
of the great advantages of working among the colored people in the centers of population, for they
are constantly coming and going.

When, a year ago, the writer received a hearty
English welcome, on the first Sunday spent in England, in the charming little vicarage nestling
among daisy-eyed fields and green hills at
Prestbury, the first familiar face that he saw as
he looked from the pulpit of the lovely old Parish
Church was a black one.   One of the parishioners
of S. Mary's had several years before left Baltimore
for the West Indies, and now unexpectedly appeared
to greet him.   Best of all, the vicar—now alas !
driven by persecution from the beautiful home of
his boyhood—declared she was one of his most ex-
emplary and devout communicants.

On Sundays, after the early celebrations, morn-

---

* A good example in this respect is set them by Mount
Calvary Church, which reports 475 communicants, and where
the average number of communicants each Sunday at the
early celebrations is about 85.

ing prayer and sermon follow at 11 o'clock. The Sunday-school, at the close of its session in the basement, assembles in the church at 4 P.M. for a short musical service and public catechising. At 8 P.M. a shortened form of evening prayer is sung, followed by a sermon. The chants used are Gregorian (Doran and Nottingham*), the hymns are set to inspiriting tunes, interspersed at night with those familiar to the Methodists, such as "Coronation," "There is a Fountain," or "Nearer, my God, to Thee." On High Festivals, more difficult music is rendered, the Communion Services of B. Tours, Monk, Mac Farran, or Schubert, while at the offertory are introduced the "Alleluia Chorus," the Gloria of Mozart's Twelfth Mass, or "Mighty Jehovah." The surpliced choir is under the direction of Mr. C. A. Johnson, our organist, and leader also of the "Monumental Band and Orchestra," who kindly furnish us an instrumental accompaniment on the chief festivals. On such occasions, so far as the number of available clergy permits, the ritual is more ornate, especially at the Solemn Celebration. Although even such services are quite plain as compared with those of many of the English churches, or some in our own country that have led in the restoration of Catholic usages, yet as far as possible the church's seasons are appropriately marked, and the services rendered attractive by banners, lights, flowers and a well ordered service.

* The excellent American edition lately published by James Pott & Co.

Doubtless, as has been often claimed by writers on the subject, an ornate ritual is especially adapted to the temperament of the colored people, and a dry wearisome service repels them. But the work of Christian grace in the hearts of these people cannot be accomplished by music or ritual. A bright service will help to draw people within the reach of instruction, and will be always loved and prized by those of any race or condition who have learned to make it the expression of earnest devotion, but permanent success in affecting the lives of the people and saving souls must be sought by deeper methods. The fearless and full presentation of sacramental teaching, the use, when needed and voluntarily sought, of confession and priestly absolution, the frequent and carefully prepared communions, the constant unwearying work of the sisters among the people, the requirement of obedience to God's laws as the test of true religion, are among the distinctive features of Catholic teaching upon which have been placed confidence in building up Christian character among them. So may the Church do for the negro what a religion in which the element of excitement and highly wrought feeling prevails can never do. God forbid that we should fail to recognize the great work done by those religious systems which have prevailed among them while the Church has so sadly neglected them. Without that work they might have been worse than heathen. Those who know them can testify that many an old Baptist brother or Methodist sister, though they have gone "shouting to glory," have gone with a pure heart and undefiled life. No good is done to the cause of religion or of truth by an indiscriminate denunciation of such forms of religion as they have known. But as loyal children of the Catholic and Apostolic Church, we must believe that she can show "a more excellent way," and the more thoughtful among themselves are recognizing the fact that the need of Christian morality, as the basis of any true service of GOD, has often been lost sight of in a religion which was too apt to mistake the loudest shouter for the highest saint.

In proportion to the length of time that they have led the lives of regular, faithful communicants, we find is overcome the tendency to seasons of "back-sliding," and periods of religious indifference, a tendency partly owing no doubt to past religious training, but also, we believe, to a shiftlessness and lack of will-power, that to a great extent still characterize them as a people. These traits it may be expected will in turn be remedied by Christian training and education, enforcement of civil laws, and the fuller appreciation of their personal responsibility in their condition of freedom. Their advance thus far gives no cause for despondency.

To awaken them from these seasons of lukewarmness, services of a more special and exceptional character have at times been successfully resorted to. As the early Church substituted Chris-

tian festivals for heathen holidays, so the Church in
the same wise and conciliatory spirit may wean the
colored people from the excesses of "Revivalism,"
by adapting herself to their ways while yet leading them to a higher life. Of such a character is
the preaching of "missions." Two "Ten-days
Missions" have been given at S. Mary's, one in the
first years of the work by the Rev. A. G. Mortimer,
another, more recently, conducted by the Rev.
George C. Betts. The immediate results of a mission are no real test of the good accomplished,
which will only be revealed at the Last Day. We
have every reason to believe, however, that God
blessed both these efforts for converting souls to
His service, both by adding to the number of communicants and by awakening to new life and zeal
those who were such already.

An example of an effort to interest the people, of quite another sort, are the parish festivals.
The first which we kept, S. Matthew's Day, 1882,
commemorated the tenth anniversary of the first
service at S. Mary's. There was a bright service
in church and a stirring sermon from the Rev. B.
W. Maturin, S. S. J. E. A bounteous supper was
then served in the school-rooms. The Hon. B. K.
Bruce, that most distinguished representative of his
race, presided, while at the guest table were a number of clergy and other distinguished guests, both
white and colored, the ladies not failing to adorn
the occasion, not only the wives of the distinguished president and speakers, but those who

6

were quite as distinctly not of the colored people, as Mrs. Charlotte Johnson (daughter of a distinguished Virginian), Mrs. Barry, and others. The presence of the Baltimore Rifles, in uniform, added to the gayety of the scene. Mr. Bruce, after a happy little speech, called on Mr. Langston, U. S. Minister to Hayti, and others of the guests to respond to sentiments, and at midnight the bell called all to the church to give thanks for a very happy festal day in a solemn Te Deum.

Another parish festival has just been celebrated, when as president of the supper we were favored with the presence of that staunch churchman as well as highly esteemed physician Dr. A. T. Augusta, while among the preachers and speakers were the Dean of Baltimore, Dr. Rich, Rev. Drs. Fair and Hyland, Rev. S. C. Stokes, Rev. H. C. Bishop of Charleston, Rev. J. B. Massiah of Newark, and others.

There are frequent entertainments of a less formal character for the purpose of social intercourse, such as suppers conducted by the female parochial societies. The Saint Faith's Guild of Schoolgirls and the Young Women's Guild of S. Mary the Virgin, have their little teas arranged by the Sisters. S. Mary's Young Men's Guild has conducted several successful entertaintments, dramatic, literary, or musical, and under two successive and faithful Guild Masters, Mr. R. A. Blay and Mr. W. E. Tilghman, have done something toward uniting the young men in the work of the parish. On the

whole it must be admitted that the result of Guild
and Society work has not been all that had been
hoped for. The great irregularity of the colored
people in attending meetings or performing prescribed duties, partly owing to the nature of their
employments but still more from lack of sense of
personal responsibility, and their tendency to petty
jealousies are among the causes which it is hoped
time will somewhat remove.

The details given convey a very inadequate
idea of our method of work, yet it is hoped it may
be of some service as a guide to many who have
asked to know it. Those of our readers who can
come and see for themselves may be sure of a hearty
welcome.

The church building is now complete in its main
features, and, except a trifling sum, being rapidly
paid, is free of all debt. It is sufficiently beautiful, especially in the appointments of the chancel,
to teach that it is for the glory of GOD, and not
erected chiefly with the thought of the convenience
of worshipers, nor made poor because their own
homes are necessarily so. Some wall decoration
and additional stained glass, some casing and plas-
tering in the school-rooms, and similar "finishing
touches" are needed for its entire completion. This
will all doubtless be provided by the voluntary
offerings which it has been found the congregation
readily supply for the perfecting of a building
which they regard with an honest pride and an
earnest affection. Already a "nest egg" is laid

by toward a reredos in which can be placed a marble panel representing in basso relievo the Adoration of the Magi, the work and generous gift to S. Mary's of the colored artist residing at Rome, Miss Edmonia Lewis. Too long it has lain in its packing box, but we felt bound to pay all our honest debts before carrying on the work of ornamentation. Among a people imaginative by nature, and many of whom read with difficulty, it would doubtless be useful to use well executed designs of Scripture scenes, or other pictorial decoration. We confess we have sometimes indulged in an ambitious dream of seeing upon the walls of S. Mary's two scenes from the life of one of the martyrs of our own communion. The first scene should represent young Patterson standing on the shore of that South Sea island, his arms about the necks of the two naked, black savages at his side, while he watched the white-winged ship sail away to that English home he had left forever. The second should be of the martyred Bishop, his body pierced with five wounds and the palm branches crossed above him, floating toward his disciples in that lonely boat. The teaching of such a life, the living for others and not for self, surely would not be lost if thus kept before the colored people of the United States.

HOME FROM MARKET.

From a pencil sketch by a communicant of St. Mary's Church.

CHAPTER IV.

THE SCHOOLS.

CHRISTIAN education has formed a prominent feature in the work of S. Mary's Chapel. In the schools have been met the greatest successes as well as the greatest discouragements and disappointments.

The permanence of any work of our Church among the colored people will largely depend upon church schools. The earlier work of our Church among them was severely censured for too exclusively pressing educational work. From these censures, as well perhaps as from their own reports, it would appear that while the general principle was a good one, they made some fatal mistakes in carrying it out. Schools were established where no opportunities were afforded of church services. So they become an end, not a means. Instead of concentrating funds on a few centers and establishing first class institutions, the work was spread out so thin as to be to a great extent ineffectual. In strong contrast to this weak policy of the Church have been some of the most successful efforts of other religious bodies.

"Let me take you," said a prominent colored Methodist minister in one of the largest Southern cities, as he held open the door of his carriage to the writer, " to see what your Church is doing for my people." As we drove thither, he continued, "I am a member of the English Church, I came to this country from the West Indies. After being excluded from one church after another on account of the color of my skin, I determined I would never connect myself with the Episcopal Church until it became Christian." We stopped at the door of a little building—one might almost say "shanty." We entered. An old white-headed negro greeted us warmly. He was a kindly old man, rather intelligent. He carried us to the end of the room where he had a class of the older children. These he taught during the week and acted as lay reader in this same building on Sundays. At the other end of this *Pro*-Chapel was his wife, a nice old aunty with Madras kerchief on her head, trying to teach a younger class their letters. We use the word trying advisedly, for if by accident a child sometimes called a letter by its right name the aunty was pretty sure to tell the child it was wrong. This faithful, devout, but ignorant old pair were two who appeared on the list of missionaries employed by the church, and this the only mission station for the colored people in one of the largest and most influential of the cities of the South. We had tremblingly passed under a portion of the ceiling where the plaster hung threateningly like the sword of Damocles. The old man took advantage of the opportunity—he was naturally clever as well as amiable. He showed us a subscription list for the repair of the building. "We would like, Reverend, to patch that a' plasterin' and tidy up a bit with whitewash an' paint." Regretting to be unable to subscribe a larger sum, S. Mary's, Baltimore, was placed on the list for $5.00. The old man's eyes glistened with tears ; so large a sum, he said, had only once before been given them— and yet the names of rectors of wealthy parishes of the city were on that list. "Come," said my guide, "let us drive where I can show you another school for my people." Again we drove together through the broad shaded avenues, while passers by looked up with scorn that two of different skins were driving together, though they were those who preached the gospel of JESUS, the Carpenter. We draw up before a stately building. Within are several hundred scholars. The higher classes are making excellent recitations in Virgil, in geometry, in literature, and from these halls, filled with neatly dressed, well disciplined and bright-faced pupils, were annually going forth teachers to every part of the State. It was not a State institution. A Methodist chaplain during the war had conceived the idea, and heartily sustained by his denomination, had built and organized this school, and was himself the principal.

As the Church's work has been chiefly planned by the rectors of Northern parishes, who have little intercourse with colored men unless as sextons of their fashionable churches, while little opportunity has been afforded those who actually labored among the colored people to suggest or in any way make their experience of service, it is not surprising that these and other still more fatal mistakes have been made. While so little was doing to relieve the real grievances which the colored people suffered at the hands of the Church, Southern sentiments were wantonly and needlessly disregarded. Some years since a lady teacher, a white woman, was employed by the Board of Missions in a city of the far South. She boarded at the house of the negro clergyman in whose parish she taught, an unpardonable error of judgment, even had he not been charged with gross misconduct. He has since been deposed. Considering the scandals connected with it—scandals well known to the clergy of the city—it was worse.

But the general principle of establishing church schools wherever work is undertaken, is a sound one. Said a colored Methodist "Bishop" to one of S. Mary's wardens: "I see my people as they become educated are leaving us. I do not wish them to become Roman Catholics. If your Church will provide for them as she ought, I would gladly advise them from my pulpit to go to you if they have made up their minds to leave us." For many years at least, it is probable that it is chiefly this better educated portion of the colored people that the Church will win. At some future time great masses of the people may be ready to come to her. In one notable instance in Virginia it is claimed they are so ready. There have been some remark-

able signs of late of seeking Holy Orders from the
Church in the body known as the " A. M. E.
Church," although this originated with the most
intelligent among their "Bishops" and preachers.
Allowing for these exceptions, probably in the
country parts and certainly in the cities—where our
experience leads us to speak with more certainty—
it will be the more intelligent element that will be
drawn to the Church. The school, therefore, pre-
pares the soil from which the young generation of
the Church will grow.

Moreover, the colored people are very ambitious
for their children, generally grateful to those who
benefit them, and, in spite of the assertion of many
to the contrary, they are very fond of them. Hence
not only are the children in such schools educated
in the Church's ways, but through the children the
parents are drawn to her. We do not think we
should err in estimating considerably more than
one-half of the increase of S. Mary's congregation
as the result of our schools. At the very beginning
of our work a parish school was established. It
was begun in the basement of the church, on the
13th of Sept., 1873, with twenty-nine boys and thirty
girls. From the first, pupils have been charged a
small tuition fee, averaging ten cents weekly. That
is lightly esteemed for which nothing is paid. All
fellow workers among the colored people whom we
have consulted agree that it is best not to make the
schools absolutely free.

At first, the clergy took turns in acting as principal, the heavier burden of work falling to Mr. Leeson, indefatigable in his labors. One of the Sisters superintended the girls' department. Ladies came in at various hours to assist. It was, however, found undesirable to continue the school in this way. Kind as the volunteer service was, it was irregular, and the constant change of teachers disorganized the school. The parochial work increased so rapidly that the clergy could not give the needed time to school teaching. After a number of experiments it has been found best to accept the services of only such volunteers as can give with entire regularity definite hours of the week, and so take exclusive charge of specified studies. Several Mount Calvary ladies still teach in the school in this way with greatest benefit both to the minds and the hearts of their pupils. One deserves especial notice, as from the very opening of the school having given her services daily, and for the whole day, as a labor of love. Surely the labors of those kind friends will not be forgotten when the Master cometh with His reward with Him.

Where a fixed salary has been given, it has, as a rule, been found best to secure colored teachers. Others usually connect an idea of degradation with teaching colored children, and accept the task only when other employment fails. Children quickly detect this spirit, and are neither respectful nor studious under them.

Soon after opening our schools a house was rented for a boarding school for girls. Many colored men

in the South at that time held important and lucrative positions. They were sending their daughters
North to be educated in schools, most of which
were under influences very hostile to our Church,
in some cases hostile to all Christian teaching.

The establishment of this school troubled some
of the truest friends of our work, and called forth
bitter censure from others less friendly disposed.
That colored girls should be taught music, French,
and Latin was contrary to all their convictions.
It did not occur to them that even if these studies
had not been to the girls' advantage, their parents
had the means and the desire to obtain such an
education for them, and that it was vastly better
that they should receive it under the restraining,
conservative influence of the Church, and in a
school where they were permitted only to advance
step by step as rapidly as they could advance
thoroughly, than in the irreligious institutions established chiefly for political ends, or in schools where
a superficial education was garnished by a smatter-
ing of instruction in wax flowers and gaudy needle-
work. Besides, we must deal with hard facts.
There were at that time colored men, not only as
now in all the professions, but al-o United States
senators and members of Congress. Whatever
one's theories on the subject, is it to be expected or
desired that such men or their families should remain ignorant? Would those who consider it a
stain upon the honor of their country to see any
but a white man sitting in the Senate, or placing

his signature upon the paper currency, feel less humiliated if instead of being gentlemanly in deportment, and occupying the position with dignity and ability, he had been an illiterate boor? Is it to be wished that he had selected for his wife, in whose drawing-room must be seen the ladies of the White House, and who mingles with the highest of the land in state receptions, an ignorant and vulgar woman instead of one whose quiet grace, gentle courtesy, and intelligent conversation have won the esteem of all who have known her? Is it well if we are to have priests from this race, who, if priests at all, must in their office be the peers of any priest, and be raised above all laymen, that they should not have wives of education and good taste to make their homes centers of refinement? So plain seemed the answers to these questions, that clergy and sisters hesitated not to establish the school. For several years it was well filled with boarders and day pupils. When political changes came in the South, by which fewer colored men held lucrative positions, it became more difficult to maintain it. A number of good schools had in the mean time been opened in the South, and our own was less needed. Death and other causes had diminished our corps of laborers, and it was difficult to maintain both the school and a boys' orphanage which had been opened in a small house which it had already outgrown. We, therefore, closed the school, and moved the boys into the house it had occupied.

But it must not be thought that the life of this

school, short as it was, was fruitless. We have had gratifying tidings of old pupils in various parts of the South. Some have become efficient teachers. Nearly all have remained steadfast Christian church women. Some have had sore trials in the difficulty of being allowed to commune where there were no special church congregations of colored people.

In the day of the boarding-school the Bishop of Hayti sent three girls of his diocese to be educated in our school. Two were long since returned to their native island as communicants of the church; the third, Miss Alice Baker, remained with us and became a most efficient teacher. She has lately returned to Hayti under appointment of the Board of Missions to teach in one of the bishop's schools. She will be greatly missed in our own work, where she has endeared herself to all.*

A number of girls, now of S. Mary's congregation, who were trained as day pupils of our school, are marked for purity of life and conversation, gentleness of manners and faithfulness to duties. Their good influence is frequently spoken of, and its genuineness can be best illustrated by a remark made by a prominent colored man of Washington, himself a Congregationalist: "You do not know, sir," he said, "how far beyond the circle of your own congregation the work of S. Mary's is felt. It used to be that in entertainments given by our people in Baltimore, a young man might be talking to a perfectly respectable girl, with low-necked

* See note on last page.

dress, resting his hand upon her bare shoulder un-rebuked. But it is often said by our young men in Washington that you cannot now do that on account of the example of the S. Mary's girls."

The boys' school has had a still more varied history. Owing to the difficulty of holding both boys' and girls' schools in the crowded basement, before the enlargement of the church, a house was rented with the expectation of a clergyman undertaking a boys' boarding as well as day school for advanced pupils. Failure of health and other reasons caused this clergyman to retire before the school was opened, leaving the house rented for three years on our hands.

In this dilemma we were so fortunate as to secure the services of a young man who desired eventually to study for the ministry, but in the mean time was glad to engage in church work, without other remuneration than "board and lodging." Mr. Charles C. Quin for three years efficiently and earnestly taught the school in the house, 180 W. Biddle Street. His courtesy and kindness to the people caused him to be as much beloved by them as he was prized by the clergy. Having out of kindness prolonged his stay beyond his original intention, he went to North Carolina to fulfill his long cherished wish of receiving Holy Orders, where he remains doing faithful work.

When we first embarked in Christian education, zealous friends supplied us with a number of general principles for our guidance, e. g. :

"Colored children are quite precocious to a certain point, beyond which it is impossible to educate them."

"If there are any very bright pupils in a school, it will be sure to be traceable to white blood in their veins."

"Only the blacks will have the necessary endurance for education. The admixture of white blood weakens body and mind."

These are mere samples. After twelve years experience of a school of from one hundred to two hundred children, none of those rules seem to "work." Practical experience is the best mode of exploding such theories, which can be pretty much reduced to the simple proposition that in the matter of mental training, colored children are much like any other children under the same circumstances.

It may perhaps be laid down as a rule—though we have found some apparent exceptions—that the imaginative faculties are more strongly developed in the negro than the logical. The power of memory is also strong. They are more likely in the future to produce historians, poets, artists and musicians than mathematicians and philosophers. They are more likely to furnish Darwins than Bacons, inventors than patient investigators. As for determining any fixed laws of mental progress by a color test, there are not yet sufficient recorded data for such generalizations. Of the two pupils who advanced farthest in S. Mary's schools, *i. e.*

through Virgil, Cicero's orations, algebra, and so on, one was lighter than most white men, with blue eyes and straight flaxen hair, the other's face would hardly have shown a mark upon it from charcoal. They kept pretty even pace while in the school. The former was quicker, the latter the more steady plodder, and it is possible this will be found to be a usual difference between the mulatto and the black. But we would not venture the assertion without further corroboration. While among both the blacks and mulattoes there were such encouraging pupils, there were naturally others equally impervious to ideas.

We trust one honest fellow will pardon our using him as an example. He has since turned out a good, steady, upright workman. His schoolmates —after the manner of boys—nick-named him the "india-rubber boy." There seemed to be no bones or fixed joints in his body. When G. was asked a question he would begin to wriggle. First he would shuffle his feet, then his ankles would begin to twist, then his legs to writhe, finally when arms, legs and whole body were going through painful contortions and gyrations, out would pop the answer from his mouth with a sort of explosive force of desperation as if from an air-gun. But the answer thus painfully worked out was not always satisfactory. For G. had a way of mastering one long word, the first that struck his fancy, early in the day. This was made to do service in answering all subsequent questions of a puzzling character. On one occasion, when he had just finished his geography recitation, he was called in the history class to give the name of one of the Presidents of the United States. He began to writhe with unwonted energy, at last, after seeming to wriggle up from his feet the whole length of his body, out popped the unexpected answer, "Archipelago, sir."

But our pupils were not all like G., though we have found many through whose long-darkened intellects it was slow work to diffuse light. We have, however, carefully compared our schools with those attended chiefly by children of the laboring class, both in this country and in England, and we believe they would not compare unfavorably. As less likely to be considered prejudiced in their favor on so important a question, we give the opinion of the chairman of the Diocesan Committee on Education:

RECTORY, CHURCH OF THE REDEEMER, }
Charles Street Avenue, }
July 20, 1880. }

REVEREND AND DEAR BROTHER:

Having attended, as a member of the Committee of Religious Instruction of the Diocese, the examinations of your Schools for Colored Boys, 1 want to say to you how much impressed I was with the results of your work.

I saw enough, I thought, to solve the doubts of any one concerning the capability of the colored race for intellectual attainment. I am sure, at least, the mistakes made by the boys were as few, and the results of the examinations were as good, as would have been found in any school of the same grade in the city.

The readiness and accuracy with which the boys told the prominent facts of the history of the country, and with which they worked out at the blackboard even quite complicated questions in arithmetic, were noteworthy; but I was especially gratified to observe that in such studies as English grammar, for instance, they made an effort to *think*— as good and as successful as I have been able elsewhere to see.

The discipline of the school was excellent, and the bearing of the boys as modest and respectful as could have been desired ; and I most cheerfully say to you that I should consider it a downright misfortune to the Church if the experiment which you seem to be making so successfully in behalf of the race should fail for lack of support or encouragement.

Yours truly,

GEO. C. STOKES.

REV. CALBRAITH B. PERRY.

The Dean of Baltimore, himself an experienced and successful teacher, having on a number of occasions attended our examinations, expressed the like opinion, while Bishop Whipple wrote, in 1870, " During my recent visit to Baltimore I visited the schools under the care of the Rev. Calbraith B. Perry and the Sisters of S. Mary's. I was much pleased with the schools. It seemed to me an honest effort to grapple with and do the work for this people in the self-sacrificing spirit of Christian love."

At the opening of our school at adjoining desks in the front row sat three intelligent boys. They were often spoken of as illustrating, not the " un-

sectarian character" of the school (as the phrase
goes), we never boasted of that, but the diversity in
religious faith of its pupils. One was the lay server
at our own altar; another, sanctuary-boy at S.
Francis', the Roman Catholic church for colored
people; the third, the son of a Methodist minister.
The last that was heard of the preacher's boy was
in the State Penitentiary. The others have had a
more creditable career. The "sanctuary-boy" removed with his family to Philadelphia. Devotedly
attached to his mother, a devout Romanist, who
well deserved his affection, he regularly attended
church with her, until one day he said, "Mother, I
have reached an age when I must think for myself.
I attended S. Mary's school too long to be satisfied
to remain in your Church. I wish to find an Episcopal Church with which to connect myself." The
mother, of course, regretted his choice, but she herself, while living in Baltimore, had become very
fond of S. Mary's, and did not seek to dissuade him.
He has ever since remained faithful in the communion of his choice. He became a messenger boy
in the United States Signal Service Office, and so
approved himself to his employer that when the
latter was appointed to a position in the water-
works, he took the lad with him, and promoted
him. He now, after his hard day's work, devotes
his evenings to study at the Franklin Institute, and
bids fair to make a successful mechanical engineer,
an honorable, as he has already become an industrious and conscientious man.

Our own server, the son of our senior warden, and brother of the Mrs. Mason whose earnest work has been recorded in a previous chapter, from an early age desired to enter the ministry.

When he and a schoolmate who had the same purpose reached the highest grade of our school, it became a question where they should complete their education. Their friends had not the means to send them to Harvard or other Northern institutions which were occasionally graduating colored men. The Church made no provision for them. Just at this time Prof. Babbitt, then of the University of South Carolina, whom the Priest in charge happened to be visiting, promised them a welcome at Columbia, and they were cordially received by professors and students, both white and colored. A few months later the University was closed. The young men returned to Baltimore greatly disheartened. One of them, Bishop, the server of whom we have spoken, was still ready to persevere. His companion abandoned his purpose and became a school-teacher. Bishop Whittingham, ever ready with counsel and encouragement, advised entering young Bishop at S. Stephen's, Annandale. We regret to say its officers were not then ready to open its doors to colored students. We understand they now act on a more liberal policy, and we make no further reflection on the events of the past which added to our discouragement and kindled the indignation of the Bishop of Maryland.

No choice seemed left but to prepare the young

man at home, as best could be done, for the Seminary. Kindly aided at times by others, Prof. Witte
of Baltimore, and Mr. Schaefer, now a highly esteemed teacher in Charleston, S. C., but then a Harvard
undergraduate, the clergy conducted him through
his studies until he was prepared to present himself to the chaplains of the Diocese for examination in all the studies prescribed by Canon. He
passed successfully, complimented by his examin-
ers, and was admitted a candidate for Priest's
Orders by the Standing Committee of Maryland.
He entered the General Theological Seminary in
New York, the first colored student to enter, as
well, it is believed, as the first to apply since Mr.
Alexander Crummel, now the Rev. Dr. Crummel
of Washington, had been refused admission some
forty years before.

It deserves to be recorded that Mr. Bishop
not only received a cordial welcome from the
Faculty and the Dean, the present Bishop of
Springfield, as well as from his successor, but also
from his fellow students. When the attention of
the Church was called to the expediency of establishing special institutions for the theological
education of colored men, a memorial was prepared
and signed by the Seminary students, candidates
from Southern Dioceses taking the lead, setting
forth the willingness to cordially welcome colored
candidates to the existing Seminaries and Theological schools, and the consequent uselessness and
inexpediency of establishing special institutions

for the purpose, at additional cost to the Church
and with necessarily less advantages to the candidates.

Mr. Bishop had grown up with the idea of assisting after his ordination at S. Mary's. At that
time he inclined to make school teaching his especial future work. This was one cause of so long
retaining the house on Biddle Street, ill-adapted to
its use as a day school, but admirably situated for
a boarding school, which it was intended to open
as soon as Mr. Bishop should return to be its
principal.

Mr. Bishop, having completed the full course of
study and graduated, returned to Baltimore to be
Ordained. But many more were the discouragements to be met by this young man in entering
the Ministry of a Church where so often has been
deplored the lack of colored clergy. A mistake
had been made in registering Mr. Bishop's name
at the time he applied to Bishop Whittingham as
Postulant. Although the name had been correct-
ly reported at conventions during the three years he
was a candidate, there was a delay of some months
until the Standing Committee should satisfy
themselves that Hutchens Chew Bishop was the
same person as Hutchens Smith Bishop. In the
meantime he quietly taught the school, having
succeeded Mr. Quin. After their next meeting it
somehow transpired that no action had been taken
upon the papers which had appeared to be at fault
only in this confusion of name. They were care-

fully drawn in the prescribed form, the one signed
as the Canon directed by the Rector and Vestry of
Mount Calvary Church, the parish from which
Mr. Bishop went to the Seminary; the other by
the Rev. Dr. Hodges, Rector of S. Paul's Church,
and by the Rev. Dr. Richey, Prof. of Ecclesiastical
History in the General Seminary. In response to
Mr. Bishop's inquiries addressed to the Standing
Committee through their Secretary, it could only
be learned that the testimonials were "not satisfactory." No hint could be obtained how they
could be made satisfactory, or in what respect they
were not already so. Nor were inquiries addressed to Bishop Pinkney more successful. He replied, "I am not admitted to their council board.
All that I know is what you know full as well."
Subsequent events seemed to exonerate the Bishop
from any desire on his own part to block Mr.
Bishop's way. The Bishop had expressed an affectionate interest in his course at an earlier stage.
He had always known and esteemed his father and
his grandfather before him. He wrote, in reply to
a respectful but earnest appeal from Mr. Bishop's
father, "I truly sympathize with you in your dis-
appointment, and regret that the Standing Committee felt obliged to so act, and would do anything in my power to gratify you in this or any
other matter, for I have much regard for you and
your father, and remember most pleasantly his constant kindness to me in years gone by. But,"
he added, "I cannot do anything to promote your

wishes in this matter." The Bishop had shown much interest in the work of S. Mary's itself, had himself handsomely contributed to its erection, and when it was nearly completed, one night, after a service held there, while quietly smoking in the study of our Clergy House, had experienced much gratification at the part the colored people had themselves taken in building the church. Amused at hearing of a friendly rivalry between the two wardens, one of whom was earnestly collecting funds to put glass in one of the large transept windows then filled with muslin, because the window on the side where the senior warden usually sat was already filled, the Bishop promptly said, " Tell your warden to give the money he has collected toward the debt on the building. I will send you $50 with which to put in the glass." When after his Ordination to the Priesthood in another Diocese Mr. Bishop sought readmission to Maryland, the Bishop received him without any hesitation, and the last official communication with the Priest in charge of S. Mary's was a letter to carry to Europe. It is so pleasant to remember as his last act after all that had passed, that it is given here in order to do full justice to the Bishop's kind heart and courtesy.

WASHINGTON, D. C., U. S. A.
March 6, 1883.

The Rev. Calbraith B. Perry is a Presbyter of the Diocese of Maryland, and at this time associated with the work of Mount Calvary Church in the city of Baltimore. He is a gentleman of fine culture, able, and of fervid zeal, and is highly esteemed for his many virtues, and by no one more than myself. Any civility shown to him during his sojourn abroad will be regarded as a personal favor to me.

WILLIAM PINKNEY,
Bishop of Maryland.

[SEAL.]

Although this letter drew a picture which was quite an objection in using it, lest the contrast with the original should become too conspicuous, yet its kind expressions could not but be prized by the possessor as a proof that its writer had no such personal feeling toward him or his work as some were wont to intimate. The fact seemed simply to be (so far as the Bishop was concerned), that he had no information in regard to the action of the Standing Committee whatsoever—although the secretary of that committee had referred Mr. Bishop to the Bishop " to learn from him what the Standing Committee had done—*the reason for their action*—and what he (Mr. B.) was to do"—and that with his peculiar notions as to the sovereign powers of the Standing Committee, he felt neither liberty to act nor to inquire into their action. Although he showed irritation when further pressed, and utterly refused to advise his candidate what to do, there was nothing in his action which could be construed as unfriendly to Mr. Bishop.

While some were confident that the real reason which the Standing Committee kept as impenetrable a mystery as the Egyptian Sphinx, was an unwillingness to receive the signatures of the clergy who had signed the papers—owing to so-called Ritualistic tendencies—ohters believed that the question of color was the real one. Some of the oldest Maryland clergy not immediately interested in the matter have always maintained this opinion. But in a question which clad itself in such Eleusinian secrecy, and which has ceased to be of any practical interest, it is perhaps best not to waste conjecture. Sufficient has been said to explain a strong and intense feeling of indignation and suspicion of offended rights on the part of S. Mary's congregation and the colored people generally. This found expression in resolutions adopted at a meeting of the colored people, which, however, called forth no more response than the previous communications. The belief has remained deeply rooted in the mind of the colored people throughout the city. The fact has been gleefully proclaimed by those hostile to the Church, and who are glad to argue that she was too aristocratic to wish to admit the Negro.

The difficulty itself was solved by the kindness of the Bishop of Albany, who received Mr. Bishop into his diocese by letter of transfer from Bishop Pinkney. He was ordained on Sunday, April 3d, by Bishop Doane, in his cathedral, the very same papers that the Maryland Standing Committee had declined to pass having been approved by the Standing Committee of Albany. Sunday evening he preached by invitation of the Rev. Dr. Harrison, at S. Paul's Church, Troy. The cordial hospitality he

received at both the Episcopal residence and at
Dr. Harrison's, the presence of his friends and relatives and the kindly words of sympathy of eminent laymen of that fine old city did much to relieve him of the feeling of being an outcast from a
diocese he had loved, and in which with filial
loyalty he desired to labor. For a time Mr. Bishop
served parishes in the northern part of New York,
by his Bishop's appointment. But the difficulties
of longer supplying his place in S. Mary's Boys'
Academy caused Bishop Doane to send him to
finish out the term of his diaconate in Baltimore,
and while not permitted to officiate ministerially,
he resumed his school duties. Although, after
his ordination to the priesthood, he was received
by the Bishop of Maryland, enough had occurred
to account for his hesitation about remaining per-
manently in the diocese. The difficulties of a young
colored clergyman starting out to work among his
race, with the natural suspicion encountered from
both white and colored people, the difficulty of any
young man doing priestly work in a congregation
where he had grown up as a boy, even if always
respected, as it was universally allowed Mr. Bishop
had been, were greatly increased in his case by the
additional difficulties we have narrated. The
school during these delays and changes had suffered and Mr. Bishop found the task of building
it up less agreeable than he had anticipated. The
Mission in South Baltimore, of which he took special charge, struggled on with few friends and en-

couragements. It is not surprising, therefore, that after remaining to assist in the work while the priest in charge took a holiday in Europe, he afterward, with the regretful but full consent of the latter, accepted a call to Charleston, and has succeeded at S. Marks his old friend at Columbia, Mr. Saltus, who has been cut off in the beginning of a promising and meritorious career. At Charleston Mr. Bishop has received a welcome that well accords with the long-established reputation of the congregation to which he has gone, and so another fledgeling has flown from the ecclesiastical nest at S. Mary's, and is the fourth of the clergy who may to a greater or less extent be claimed as her offspring.

Hardly more brief could have been made the details of a painful chapter of the history of S. Mary's, too intimately connected with her struggles to be omitted. The Academy in the meantime had suffered from these changes. For years it had been with difficulty kept waiting for Mr. Bishop's return. It had in the meantime not been without advantages. The Rev. George B. Johnson, of "S. James's African Church," of Baltimore, a teacher formerly of S. Paul's School, Concord, had given his services as instructor in some of the higher branches. The clergy of the parish were also instructors in the school, and Mr. Perry D. Robinson, a young colored graduate of the admirable "Institution for the Education of Colored Youth" in Philadelphia, had been employed, first

as Mr. Bishop's substitute, then as his assistant.
On Mr. Bishop's leaving for Charleston, Mr. Robinson became Principal. He was universally esteemed by clergy and people, and thoroughly satisfactory as a teacher. But the load of carrying on
this school had become too great for the shoulders
of the clergy, or perhaps, from continual "belabor-
ing," their shoulders had begun to weaken. A
few months after Mr. Bishop's departure, the other
assistant, the Rev. J. O. Davis, was obliged to
withdraw his valuable services, and his place could
only be temporarily filled. This crippled the task
of maintaining a school for which constant appeals
for funds were necessary, and which, calling forth
little enthusiasm from white or colored people,
seemed Herculean.

The lower departments were handed over to the
Sisters, and are still continued in the basement of
the church. The house on Biddle Street was
given up. The few older boys who remained were
removed to the choir-room of the church, where
Mr. Robinson, under great difficulties, completed
the year for which he was engaged. On the 16th
of June, 1884, the scholars, joined by former pupils
who had been under Mr. Robinson's instruction,
met with their parents and friends in the basement
of the church for farewell exercises and a straw-
berry treat. It was made as happy an affair as
possible, but it was necessarily with regret and
sadness that a work on which so much labor had
been spent, so many hopes builded, was now sus-

pended. Especially did it cause pain to part with
Mr. Robinson, whose influence for good among the
young men of our work had been very marked in
addition to his excellence as a teacher. After
original essays from Masters Blay and Owens,
readings by Masters Berkly Waller and Francis,
and a dialogue by Masters Francis, Bright and
Thomas, and a "Spelling Bee," a copy of Shake-
speare was presented to Mr. Robinson with a little
farewell speech by Master Edward Adams, which,
as the last production of the school (and it is given
just as written by him without aid or correction),
may appropriately close the history of S. Mary's
Boys' Academy :

"It devolves upon me to offer you, in the name
of the Rector and pupils of S. Mary's Boys' Academy and their friends, a slight token of their esteem and regard. To myself it is a source of great
pleasure to be made their mouth-piece on this occasion. I am not now addressing you as our teacher,
but as our friend, our dear trusted friend and very
much-tried friend—for how often have we not
tried your temper and your forbearance.

"Dear teacher, we will ever keep your name en-
shrined in our hearts, and shall look back to this
school not as an abode of penance, but rather of
pleasure, since your kindness and amiability have
so rendered it, our studies having been illuminated
by your patient graciousness.

"The little gift we offer you is of no intrinsic
value, but it is rich in love, gratitude and respect.

Please accept it, and with it our united hopes that your life will ever be as happy as you have made ours."

It is not our purpose to chant a coronach over this school. It accomplished much that we trust has entered into the permanent life of S. Mary's. The portions of the schools still conducted by the Sisters, schools of about 200 pupils, are successful, and at least give the most necessary parts of education. We should have been glad to have continued the more advanced schools for boys and for girls, but they were burdens we could not longer carry. Had they been sustained as they deserved to be, they would still be in existence.

But neither will we have the discontinuance of the school interpreted as a change of conviction as to its need. Some one will yet take up this work in Baltimore and make it a success.* Two institutions are greatly needed, and if the Church is wise, either as general or diocesan institutions or by co-operation of the city parishes—for it is too much to expect of any one—she will establish

---

* Since the above lines were written we learn that the Order of S. Joseph, of which our former assistant Rev. A. B. Leeson is now Provincial, has opened for colored young men in Baltimore such an academy as we, for lack of support, have abandoned. We can only wish for the Roman Church, as for all who are ready to labor for a people who so greatly need the efforts of all, the success their efforts deserve. *Her* work is not accustomed to be abandoned for lack of means; but is it not a disgrace that our own Church is not in the field ?

them, and thus gain the influence among the colored people which will result. One is an industrial school where girls can learn house-work, needle-work and laundry-work. Nothing can be more important to the white people, as well as to the colored. Thus will be trained honest, industrious and skillful household servants, seamstresses and laundresses.

The second is such an academy as it was attempted to establish in connection with S. Mary's. One for girls would be useful. For boys it is greatly needed. Here would be gathered from all quarters under church instruction the most intelligent representatives of their people—those who were studying for special departments, as law or medicine, or mechanical pursuits, or fitting for higher colleges. From them would grow up influential laymen, and from among them the Church would be likely to cull the best material to send to her seminaries. The constant demand is made for more colored clergy. But how and where are they to get their education? The last General Convention emphatically refused to amend the Canons so as to lower the required intellectual standard for the priesthood. Such an amendment was strongly urged by the Sewanee Conference of Southern Bishops and Clergy. But many who labor among the colored people, and the writer among that number, and the great majority if not all of the colored clergy themselves, believe that such an opening of the door to an illiterate Priesthood would be fatal to the Church's work among them.

But to keep this door of a "short cut" to the ministry carefully closed, yet to give no aid to enter by the regular way, is cruel and unjust. From Mr. Bishop's case it can be seen that there is no bar to their entering our seminaries. Another, Rev. Mr. Massiah, has graduated from the General Seminary since, and there is a colored candidate there at present. The Philadelphia Divinity School has graduated several, and they have been treated with marked kindness by the Bishop of Pennsylvania, as well as by the professors and students.* But where are they to get the requisite

---

* The following information was kindly furnished by the Bishop of Pennsylvania after the above was in type. Among the names of the colored clergy which he gives appear several of those who have been exceptionally successful. This strengthens our position that educating the colored clergy in the companionship of the white and with equal advantages, is the best means of insuring their success:

EPISCOPAL ROOMS, PHILADELPHIA, *November* 6, 1884.

DEAR MR. PERRY:

The following colored persons have graduated at the Philadelphia Divinity School:

Rev. W. H. Josephus, ordained 1871. Died Nov. 19, 1873.

Rev. Joseph N. Durant, ordained 1869, Codington College, West Ind.

Rev. Henry L. Phillips, ordained 1875. Moravian Seminary, Jamaica.

diploma to be admitted as candidates for priest's orders, or the training necessary to pass the required "examination of literary qualifications"? They ask for no "dispensations" from the canonical requirements in their behalf—they only ask the opportunity of acquiring this preparation.

Writes a clergyman of a Southern diocese, one of the most earnest and self-denying of the laborers in this field of work, after expressing his dissent from the action of the late General Convention:

"And then, when thus blocking our wheels, they promised us money, and talked about $50,000. Where is the money? The only sensible course

---

Rev. Joseph L. Bryant, ordained 1879, Lincoln University.

Rev. Peter A. Morgan, ordained 1877, Lincoln University.

Rev. Paulus Moort, M.D., ordained 1882.

Rev. J. Benjamin Williams, ordained 1882.

Rev. J. Pallam Williams, ordained 1882.

Rev. Alfred C. Brown, ordained 1884, Cambridge High School, Mass.

I have also ordained the Rev. W. F. Floyd, now in Louisville, Ky., and last June, the Rev. Thomas G. Harper, King's College, London.

I have now in the school a colored candidate, William Adger, who graduated two years ago from the University of Pennsylvania. I have had many more under my care. I feel deeply for this class of men, and have done all in my power to elevate and cultivate them. In some cases I have been greatly disappointed; in others greatly comforted.

Very truly yours,

WM. BACON STEVENS.

in the work would seem to be, if colored men are to be educated priests, to provide for their education at the South in Raleigh or elsewhere; but when you demand that they shall be educated you give them no chance. Only $400 could be raised for Raleigh. What shall I do for M——? I want to get him into some school at the North. He ought to go one year to a preparatory school, and I believe he would then go through college swimmingly. You great 'sticklers' for an educated ministry ought to show your zeal now, and help forward the work. What institution bids for him? Black as black can be! Surely somebody will take him and be glad of the chance! He must get a satisfactory diploma; nothing short of Harvard will satisfy the Standing Committee, though a white man can get in with the weakest sort of an education! But, joking aside, can you help me find a place for him, as honest a man and as earnest a churchman as ever went upon this earth, but the sun has touched him very harshly. He learns easily, and is well along in his books."

It is a shame that the Church has not long since established several well endowed institutions to meet this need. There are many reasons why no better place could be found than Baltimore in which to locate one of them. But the reader must not be wearied with their enumeration.

We would add only a word in regard to one or two difficulties in this matter of education and their possible solution. It must be confessed that the character of the younger generation of colored people who have received the advantages of education is in many respects extremely disappointing. As they enter upon manhood and womanhood they betray a great distaste for labor. Unwilling to take the positions that their parents have occupied, of household servants, they do not show sufficient diligence, perseverance, and "push" to secure or retain positions of a more independent character, even when opened to them. Great half-grown men work for a little while, spend all their wages in fine clothes, pleasure excursions and entertainments, and without shame are content without contributing to the maintenance of the household, to depend upon hard-working parents, scrubbing, washing and toiling in every way for those whom they are rather pleased to see "play the gentleman," and whom they foolishly though fondly indulge. The younger generation of colored people of the best educated classes are adopting a style of living absurdly extravagant and utterly beyond their means. A young girl is offended if her gallant does not call to take her to the evening entertainment in a hired carriage. The style of dress upon the street of a Sunday afternoon is astonishing. It is not that it is in itself ugly: many of the colored people show great refinement of taste in combinations of color and form. But one wonders where the sons and daughters of hard-working mothers, who struggle to meet the monthly rent, and sometimes require alms to enable them to do so, can find

money for the rustling silks and brilliant feath-
ers, the "nobby" suits and glittering ornaments.
In a word, there is a general tendency—not without
marked and praiseworthy exceptions, we are glad
to allow—to extravagance and improvidence, combined with idleness and frivolity. There is little
appreciation of the dignity of labor; there is no
true ambition by persevering industry and judi-
cious economy to acquire fortune.

It is useless to seek the causes of all this in the
past. They can be found without looking far.
The old régime of slavery was a poor teacher of
the dignity of labor, of economy, of thrift, of ambition, or of self-respect. The sudden change to
liberty, the flattery and sentiment that have been
lavished upon the "freedman," with the neglect
of his real advancement, and many other causes,
combine to produce the condition we have described. It is not so important to seek its explanation as its remedy. It is of the greatest importance to white and colored people that the remedy
should be applied, and at once.

With Christian people it scarcely needs to be
argued that the first requisites are a thorough
training in Christian morals and the grace of God
to form and strengthen the character to live by
Christian rule. But God works by and through
human instrumentalities. The work must be
done not only by the colored man—his white
brother has his part to do.

What is required from the former is evident.

They must continue to grow manly, brave, energetic, ready to battle and to win. It is required of all people—especially is it necessary for a people struggling for existence in a land and among races like those of the United States.

But in this they need help. Indeed, since so large a portion of our population as the negro element cannot decay and perish without spreading corruption and death about them, they need, if necessary, compulsion. If need be, they must be spurred on in the race, forced by stronger wills until their own wills are strengthened.

But it is easier as well as better to draw than to push. We may push them to the wall; *up* hill we must lead them. We must present some adequate incentive if we would see them struggle up to honest, industrious effort. At present that incentive is lacking.

Some will reply, Let them be content with the position they have ever occupied. In the first place, that position no longer exists. No longer, as in the days of slavery, is a great retinue of servants attached to every gentleman's establishment. New spheres of labor must be opened to them, or perforce many must remain idle. But were this not so, in their new condition of freedom it were still necessary to furnish higher incentives to their efforts. You cannot dam a stream without causing it to stagnate and grow putrid. The artificial barrier of slavery is down. The law of mankind in unrestrained freedom is progress. Of course the great mass of the colored people—as of every people—will remain in humble positions. But the advance of those who struggle to the front keeps the whole body in healthy motion. The advance of those who have the ability to struggle cannot be impeded with impunity. But at present the progress of the colored people is artificially blocked.

With few exceptions (to be noted hereafter,) the only fields open to them are the work of the ministry and politics. No people are helped by the former being sought for the sake of personal advancement. As to politics, the reader may probably conjecture how elevating is the eager race after the few political prizes with which both parties cajole, delude and coquet with the colored race. In fact, there is hardly anything injuring the younger generation of colored men more than attention to politics. Thrown into the excitement and temptations of a political campaign, they are flattered and bribed with delusive promises to influence the votes of their people. This end accomplished, they are left to wait in idleness for the fulfillment of promises of political advancement. Generally, they wait in vain. The few prizes distributed among them are for the most part conferred upon the most unscrupulous and unworthy, since such can be most "useful."

Nearly all other avenues of honorable advancement are closed against them. The jealousy of the "trades unions" prevents their learning or practicing mechanical pursuits. Trustworthy architects and contractors have told us that no builder would dare to employ a colored carpenter, no matter how satisfactory and respectable a workman he might be. Carpenters who have attempted to apprentice colored boys have been warned by the all-powerful "unions" that they must dismiss them.

It is said to be different in some parts of the South. Where there is great scarcity of white labor, colored people may find it less difficult to obtain employment in these pursuits. Nothing breaks down prejudice like necessity. Charleston, S. C., can hardly be accused of being deeply imbued with "Northern sentiment," nor is it longer under "carpet-bag" control. Yet a friend there furnishes the names of a large number of colored men in important and lucrative positions. Not only are there twenty-five colored men on the police force, but one is a lieutenant, having command of both white and colored officers, and is "considered one of the most efficient officers on the force." Another is a magistrate. The largest dealer in fish and game is a colored man. Five tailoring establishments (one the largest in the State, the proprietor being worth about $200,000), one shoe store, one cigar manufactory, are owned and carried on by colored men. Three wholesale and retail butchers, two workers in sheet-iron, two house-builders and carpenters, two blacksmiths, two wheelwrights, four cotton-shippers, one shipbuilder, two deep-sea pilots, two companies of masters and owners of coasting vessels (the first owning six vessels), two others owning "fishing smacks," appear upon the list, while others are responsible and well-paid clerks in drug and grocery stores.

But we speak of the condition of things in Baltimore. No colored teacher is employed in the public schools of this city, even in those provided exclusively for colored children (yet there are 16,000 colored people employed as teachers in the United States, some of them surely fit to teach in the public schools of Baltimore). No prominent business house would venture to employ a colored man in any position higher than porter. They are occasionally required to do the work of shipping clerks and other responsible duties on account of their trustworthiness and experience, but without either the name or the pay. The devil is, indeed, less fastidious. Bar-rooms and gambling saloons give men good opportunities, and such positions are eagerly sought.

As we have said, there are a few exceptions. They strengthen our argument. The position of public caterer has ever afforded an opportunity for colored men to acquire a competence, and some of the most respectable and best colored men of the city are so employed. Four keep large and well patronized "provision stores." They are men regarded by their people as leaders of integrity. Two of them are vestrymen of S. James' Church.

The late John Lockes was the president of the Chesapeake Marine Railway and Dry Dock Co., the only business corporation of colored men in the city. He died worth a considerable property, and was universally liked and respected by his white acquaintances as well as by his own people. His successor in office (another vestryman of S. James' Church) is a man of like character. These exceptional cases, as well as some few others who have acquired some property, as barbers, caterers, sextons, undertakers and the like, are among the most intelligent, modest, courteous and upright men among their people. There are too few of them to exercise an extensive influence and counteract that of noisy and unscrupulous politicians.

Should not the business men and Christian philanthropists of Baltimore encourage the colored man thus to become a thrifty, honest and productive element of the community? Only by throwing open to him more of the prizes of life, only by furnishing a worthy goal for his ambition and reward for his industry, will this be attained. The capitalists who would establish a manufactory of any kind where colored men should find employment and be rewarded with honorable positions, as clerks, accountants, superintendents and the like, and ultimately with an interest in the concern when— and *only when*—they became qualified for the positions, would not only do a work of philanthropy and patriotism, but also, we believe, carry on a lucrative business. As President Haygood, of

Emory, well says, "The first thing of all to do is the simplest, yet, perhaps the most difficult—*clear the way*. Remove all hinderances; make the paths straight—not strait; give him the best chance possible. If all this were done, the problem would, by and by, solve itself. To do this, to give him this best chance possible, it is not impossible that some of us white people of the South must, first of all, put ourselves through a course of schooling in right views on this subject."

Said Senator Brown of Georgia, in the United States Senate, December 15, 1880 : "Under the slavery system the relations were kind. When the war came on it was supposed by many that they would rise in insurrection and soon disband our armies. They at no time ever behaved with more loyalty to us, or with more propriety. Since the end of the war, when, as we thought you very unwisely gave them the ballot, they have exercised the rights of freemen with a moderation that no other race would have done. Therefore I say it is our duty in the South, especially, and I think yours in the North as well, to encourage them, and, as they are now citizens, to elevate them and make them the best citizens possible."

Let this liberal sentiment prevail. Give the colored man a fair chance. Discriminate neither for nor against him. Either course is an injustice to him. Let him measure himself and under favorable circumstances discover his own weight. Let him unhampered rise to that position for which

God intended him, and be sure he will rise no higher. His *social position* is in nowise concerned in the matter. That, like every one's social position, will take care of itself. He only asks for fair play in the battle of life. Well says Rev. Dr. Marshall: *
"With no race does kindness, forbearance and justice go farther than with the negro. Could he *as a man* receive his honest dues—be fairly dealt with in every relation of life—for twenty years, he would amaze mankind with the outcome and the improvement of which he is capable."

---

* "The Colored Race Weighed in the Balance, being a reply by C. K. Marshall, D.D. of Vicksburg, Miss., to the speech of the Rev. J. L. Tucker, D.D." Dr. Marshall certainly deals some heavy blows "straight from the shoulder," not only at Dr. Tucker but at our Church. In regard to some of the charges against the Church, she has certainly laid herself open to them; as to others, he would no doubt speak more gently did he know her better. Certainly she is not, as he would seem to represent her, the great exponent of antinomianism. There is much good common sense in his book, and valuable testimony from one who evidently knows what he is talking about, as well as very much that is very cleverly and comically told.

ST. MARY'S ACADEMY

CHAPTER V.

S. MARY'S HOME.

ON the south side of Biddle Street, just beyond the Richmond market, stands a plain three-story brick house only to be distinguished from its neighbors by a small gilded cross over the door. On the door-plate may be read the words " S. Mary's Home." Here, unobtrusively and quietly, is carried on one of the most important of the departments of our work. Ring the bell; a sister probably will open the door. Her habit, her distinctive dress, may be recognized as that of the All Saints' Sisters of the Poor. Two of these sisters reside at the house. One of the two is the sister in charge of the work carried on among the colored people. On entering, you may encounter another sister, whose dark face, beneath the neat white cap, may be a surprise, and whose habit of dark blue, may suggest the name of her Order. This is a sister of S. Mary's and All Saints. When S. Mary's was begun, one of the most effective instruments of the spread of the Roman Catholics among the colored people in Baltimore was a large and successful sisterhood of their own race. The mother-house of the Order is in Baltimore. Branch houses are established in several cities of the South. Their visiting from house to house has been the means of converting large numbers to their communion. Their care of the sick was deservedly praised; while a large boarding and day school for girls, receiving pupils from all parts of the country, furnished, if not in every respect, a thorough and useful education, yet an attractive one, embroidery and music holding prominent places, and gained them a great influence not only in Baltimore, but throughout the land. It was felt that if our own Church would win this people she must not be content with jealous eye to look askance at such a power, or, in idleness, to expend her strength in loud-mouthed lamentations over the "spread of popery," but, giving all credit and well-earned praise for the labors of others, must emulate their zeal by using similar means to propagate, as we believe, a purer faith and practice. With this intent, the establishing of a colored sisterhood was undertaken, and in the year 1876 the first sister was received as a novice, and at the expiration of her five-years' novitiate "professed" or admitted full sister—the first colored sister, it is believed, in the Anglican Communion. There are now two full sisters, one novice and one postulant. The growth of such an Order is necessarily slow. The novitiate is unusually long, that it may give time to "make full proof of their ministry." There is special need to guard against its becoming an asylum for those merely seeking a home and support. There is often need of further instruction than simply in the "rule" and life of a Sister. It may therefore be many years before there will be the number needed for our own local work, to say nothing of responding to the calls that already come from home and abroad for colored Sisters. Clergy who come in contact with colored people could do much to hasten this time if they would keep the subject before them, and make known to them that there is such a sisterhood where those may be received who are called of God to the noble work of loving self-sacrifice.

But only the threshold of the Home has been reached. On entering, to the left hand is a neat though plain reception-room. As one rests a moment before going over the house, there may be heard merry laughter and noisy shouts through the closed folding-doors. It is quite possible there may be sounds quite the reverse of laughter, and some not altogether amiable words from childish lips, for we are not about to introduce to the reader cherubs or the "good boys" of Sunday-school books. But there they are, tumbling about in comfortable yet controlled freedom, a dozen or more little fellows, most of them with curly heads and black faces, in which glisten bright eyes and white teeth—the younger boys of the Orphanage. Through another open door, if it happens not to be during school hours, will be seen in the long yard, which extends back to Howard Street, a dozen or so of the older boys playing with their tops or with ball and bat. Here are sheltered a score of little colored boys from four to twelve years old, otherwise homeless or rescued from houses of wretchedness, clothed, fed, educated in the parish day school, and, best of all, lovingly taught to grow up as Christian men, and therefore useful citizens. How is this institution supported? is often asked. Invariably the reply has to be made, "We do not know, except that God provides for it." It is a marvel to ourselves that the end of each year finds the Home without debt. It is a fulfillment of the promise, "Dwell in the land and be doing good, and verily thou shalt be fed."

The Home was undertaken at the earnest solicitation of the colored people themselves. There was no shelter or orphanage for colored boys of any description in the State of Maryland except a reformatory institution. It was said to be not uncommon for parents or guardians of children left without support to cause them to commit some petty crime in order to have them sentenced to the Reform School. It is an excellent institution for its purpose, established and superintended by charitable and influential citizens because before its establishment there was no place to send juvenile colored offenders except the city jail. But a reform school is no place for innocent children. When, urged by the representations of the colored people, we announced our intention to open a Boys' Home, a public meeting was held enthusiastically indorsing the movement, when several of the colored Methodist ministers and other prominent colored men made stirring appeals. The yearly rent was pledged and a hearty support. But "out of sight, out of mind." Within a few months nearly all the subscriptions failed. The quiet work was not of a character to keep up an enthusiasm, and with the exception of a very few, some within and still fewer without S. Mary's congregation, the colored people show little concern about its necessities. They have not yet learned to encourage movements in their behalf.

This house is rented for $500 a year. The rent is partly met by the income of the day school, the weekly ten-cent payments from each pupil; the Sisters teach in the school without other remuneration. For the rest of the rent, just as the prospect darkens, and the time that it is due draws near, some kind friend, most often unsolicited, sends five or ten dollars to the Sisters' relief. To our shame, in this country, be it said, it is quite as often a pound from friends in England as five dollars from those near home.

Every day a Sister goes out with basket over her arm, through the markets, and into shops, and receives what the dealers choose to give her. If it were not contrary to their traditions, there could be pictured the English homes of refinement, and in some cases of luxury, which they have given up in order to come to a strange land, to live in common as Sisters with those of a long despised race, to be as mothers to fatherless little ones, and to live upon the charity of those who fill the baskets which they themselves carry through the markets, and from door to door, a contrast which, in itself, teaches what self-sacrifice the service and love of Christ can call forth.

To the credit of the marketmen be it said, that however slow the wealthy are in being moved by this example, it is not lost upon the butcher and greengrocer at his stall. The basket never goes home empty. With a cheery smile, one after another throws in a chop or bit of steak, two or three potatoes, or a handful of fruit. Except that the colored people themselves give one or two "pound parties" each year at the Home, all coming with their little parcels—sometimes a larger one, a bag, and once even a barrel of flour—as an offering to the good Sisters, whom they have learned to bless, and that now annually a Christmas offering is sent in paper bags, all the food is obtained by this daily begging of their bread, and so kind has been the response that there has been no lack. On the contrary, ten or twelve famished households have at times been helped by the Sisters from what they have spared from their own little store.

But as the work increases, as more Sisters are added, and the teaching of the schools and visiting of sick and poor require more time, it will be almost impossible to depend solely on this uncertain income, especially for such regular expenses as rent and fuel. It seems, too, a great pity that a much larger number of children should not be taken. They could be cared for with comparatively slight increase of labor and money.

The time must soon come, therefore, to make an effort to purchase or erect a suitable building for the Home. It can be undertaken by the weary work of gathering small sums throughout the country. But, oh! how many toilsome days and anxious nights it would save those engaged in the work, if some liberal layman or laywoman should be moved to build or purchase a suitable building for the Home. There are noble gifts, like Wolfe Hall and Shattuck Hall. There are schools and orphanages furnished by our Church for the white men on our frontiers—for the red men, for the Chinese, the Mexicans, the Greeks—but the names which will be ever gratefully remembered by the colored man as connected with generous gifts and institutions established for his improvement, such as General Armstrong and General Howard, and Mr. Slater, are not of our own household of faith.

Having visited the dormitories—airy, sunshiny rooms, with snug little cots, which are covered with bright counterpanes—one passes down the high steps of the Home into the street. Here a Sister leads a little procession of boys starting for their afternoon walk, or on their way to school or to Church. Here comes another Sister from market, with well-laden basket on arm, great mingling of scraps of meat and various odd things on top, red, green and gray, all which will be duly sorted, and make dishes not unsavory.

Behind her, two of the larger boys, Charlie and Berkley, or Albert and Tom, drag, like a goodly pair of prancing ponies, a little wagon—a toy with many children, but here serving the sensible purpose of carrying for the Sisters the overplus. A propos of Berkley and Albert, we must close our account of the Home with two episodes connected with its life.

Berkley, a quick-witted little fellow, very "light-complected," as our colored friends say, entered the Home with an older brother, not only "bright skinned" (another name for those nearly white), but very bright in mind. In his studies he rapidly outstripped all the boys of his age in the school. After a few years he was too old to longer remain in the Home. His studious habits, which had quickened his natural gifts, as well as his good conduct and zeal in religious duties, made it a matter of regret that his culture should not be carried further. Kind friends in Oxford, England, offered him an education there, while Father Benson, the Superior of the Society of S. John the Evangelist, has given him not only a home, but all of a father's care and interest. A short time ago, when the writer saw for the first time the graceful towers and quaint, crumbling archways of that shrine of scholarship, the little fellow, in his stumpy silk hat and funny little bob-tailed coat of the English school-boy, was the first to welcome him to Oxford. And it was a cause of great thankfulness to hear that not only did he lead in his sports and was a general favorite among the sturdy English boys—for his being colored has no other effect upon his companions than of giving them an unusual interest in him, so ignorant are our English cousins of our American class prejudices—but that he also excelled in his studies, and, according to the master's testimony, exercised a good influence by his example of Christian conduct. So has started the first, as we might say, of the graduates of our Home.

Connected with Albert Wahzhewakka Morgan, there is a more dramatic history. It was Easter Eve, 1880, and around the font at S. Mary's was gathered such a group as, probably, has not been seen upon our Atlantic coasts for many a long day. In snowy surplice and stole stood the commanding figure of an Indian priest. It was the Rev. J. J. Enmegahbowh, the first "red man" ordained to the ministry. Around him were gathered the clergy of S. Mary's and the little surpliced colored boys who acted as servers. Before him, at the font, knelt an Indian girl to whom he was sealing the name of Elizabeth Amelia, as from the baptismal shell he poured the regenerating drops upon her head while, at the rail of the baptistery, stood the old Christian Indian chief Minnegoshig, the English Sisters of All Saints, the colored Sisters, the young Haytian girl whom Bishop Holly had sent, and a number of the congre-

gation of S. Mary's.   It was truly a Pentecostal
scene.

About a year before this event, a ring of the
door-bell of S. Mary's Home had startled the sisters at a late hour.   On opening the door, a lady
stood there with a poor, dark and downcast-faced
girl by her side.   A dear old sister, whose sweet,
wrinkled face has become loved with almost a holy
reverence by the colored people, was at that time
in charge of the Home.   To her the lady said :
"We have brought you this poor Indian girl, sister.   We found her a homeless wanderer upon the
streets of Annapolis, in danger of falling into a
degraded life.   We knew not what to do with her.
We have brought her to you."   What could the
sister do but give her shelter ?   Yet it was a puzzle
to provide for her.   At this time the Home was
full of the boarding pupils, of whom we have
spoken.   It was doubtful if the girl was a proper
companion for them ; very ignorant, it was certain
she could not be instructed in the same classes
with them.   It was, therefore, with some misgiv-
ing that the Sister, in the morning, informed the
chaplain what she had done.   Touchingly she told
the tale.   The girl, some fourteen years before,
had been left on an Indian battle-field, one
of three little "papooses" the only living crea-
tures remaining among the bleeding corpses.
A private soldier, finding and pitying this little
thing, took her home to his wife.   For some
years they treated her with great kindness.   But

the soldier "took to drink" and in turn was taken
to prison. His wife, some years after, followed in
the course of her husband, both as to his habits
and habitation; so poor Elizabeth was homeless.
What could the chaplain say but that the Sister
could not have shut out this poor girl in the dark,
and that somehow we must make room for her.
Besides, some burning words of Bishop Whipple,
while the chaplain was yet in the Seminary, had
greatly interested him in the wronged red man,
and he has ever felt that those words have done
much in giving direction to his life. Although
God has seemed to send him with the gospel
message to another people, yet here God seemed
directly to send to him one of those in whom his
interest had been first awakened. A corner was
found for poor Chatry, as she had been called,
and, half as a house servant and half pupil,
she was carefully taught, at the same time, house
work and the elements of an education. Her
nature, at first somewhat stubborn and wayward,
and bearing many marks of the degrading associations of her life, soon yielded to the gentle teachings of the Sisters, and when she had been carefully
prepared, it was decided she should be baptized on
Easter Eve. Only an hour before the appointed
time for the service, the chaplain heard, accident-
ally as men are wont to say, but certainly prov-
identially, that an Indian clergyman was in town,
and so, hastening for him, the result was this
deeply significant group about the font.

But the part of the story that reads most like a romance—yet most touchingly true—remains yet to be told. Enmegahbowh and his old chief returned to their western home. Soon Minnegoshig's only daughter was taken from him by death. The loving and sorrowing father, remembering Elizabeth, in whom at the time of her baptism he had evinced a lively interest, made the request that she might be sent to him as his adopted daughter. We should have preferred to give her a more thorough training, but she had expressed a desire to live and labor among her people, and now God seemed to open the way, and we dared not to question His time. The Sister in charge accompanied the girl, in order to see her safely established in her new home, and was cordially welcomed and entertained by the Rev. Mr. Enmegahbowh and his wife. One can easily see that there was much of a trying nature in Elizabeth's new position, and it was not without friction at first that she adjusted herself to her changed relations, but her short life ended in victory. The end can best be related in the words of the Rev. J. A. Gilfillan, the missionary at White Earth Reservation, in a letter to the Sister received soon after her death :

"It gives me great pleasure to tell you of one whom you loved. Elizabeth was one whom grace had ripened for her early home. She was always gentle, kind and good. She was perfectly pure in her life, truthful and loving, and fulfilled every duty of life with quietness and patience. She took care, faithful care, of several sick and dying persons, dying of consumption, and was unwearied in watching with them ; sometimes being as far away as sixteen miles from this place. There was a quietness and loveliness about her disposition, and about all she did, which endeared her strongly to those who knew her. She was indeed one of God's unnoticed and unknown ones ; but great in His eyes, I believe and trust. One consumptive whom she faithfully nursed to the end was a daughter of Rev. Mr. Johnson—'Enmegahbowh.' [After referring to some of the misunderstandings and trials to which we have alluded, and to her falling ill while at the " Government House," " where the white people, good, kind people took care of her," he continues :] " Thence she was brought, at her own request, to the Bishop Whipple Hospital, adjoining my house, and there she had every care and attention that love and skill could devise. Her adopted mother came to see her there, and was with her much of the time. . . . You will see from what I have said there were some painful passages in her life. . . . Those things did her no permanent harm—were permitted in the good Providence of God and worked for her eternal good. She never regretted having come to Minnesota. Elizabeth was buried under the shadow of the Church of S. Columba, by the side of her adopted father, who had always been remarkably kind to her, and where the white people will lie who were kind to her. Hoping you may meet many such lambs in Paradise as the one you were permitted to train and send out here, and with prayers for every blessing upon you and your work, I am very respectfully your brother in the Lord.

J. A. GILFILLAN."

One such record as this is enough of reward and encouragement for those who have labored for the Home or have aided it.

On her return, the sister expressed a lively interest in the red men and shared with the chaplain the desire to be of further service to them. Shortly after, the latter, in a conversation with the Hon. Carl Schurz, then Secretary of the Interior, expressed his readiness, to take one or two Indian boys into the Orphanage, which had by that time taken the place of the boarding school. The Secretary suggested that it was not unlikely that the Government would be glad to send a large number of them to the Home, in which case there would be an appropriation made for their support, as at Hampton and Carlisle. The undertaking of this more extended work needed further consideration, as it would require increased accommodation and the employment of a greater force than the sisterhood then or now could furnish. The chaplain promising to refer this plan to the sisters, again assured the Secretary that, in any event, one or two would be gladly received into the Home. The latter inquired what amount would be expected for their support. When told that no remuneration was asked, that their care was undertaken only as an act of charity, he exclaimed. "What! you are ready to do this without pay ? You are the first man who ever entered this office and wished to work for the United States without being paid for it. You certainly deserve to have your request granted." Some months later, when it was feared the memorandum of our offer had been lost in the immense files of papers of the Indian office, a telegram was received, stating that

from a late night train a little Indian boy would
be delivered to us. He came, the silent little fellow. He was a son of an Indian interpreter, whose
dying request of the officer of the U. S. Army who
stood over him was that his boy should be brought
up in the white man's religion and the white
man's ways. So a second time did God seem to
send us one of His little ones of this long-injured
race. He was adopted as a ward of the parish, and
each year the children bring their Sunday-school
offerings to the altar on Low Sunday for the
support, at the Home, of little Albert, who, we
trust, is growing up to be of future service to his
race.

These details may help to impress upon others
our own firm conviction that, in the mission work
among the colored people, the aid of Sisters will be
found of the greatest importance, if not absolutely
essential. As in other work, the gentle, tender
ministrations of a woman, especially when devoted
wholly to such work and hence skilled in it, will
make itself felt in the sick room, in the desolate
home of the poor, in sorrow and in sin. The distinctive dress protects them in alleys and courts
which other women may not enter with equal safety
and propriety. Above these advantages, and without speaking of that other highest blessing, which
is beyond human reckoning, the answer to the frequent united prayers of such a community and to
the loving sacrifice of their service, there is another
light in which the establishment of sisterhoods is

of inestimable benefit. While the exaggerated accounts of the universal impurity, dishonesty and untruthfulness of the colored people are not true, yet as we have already admitted, that whatever may be their characteristics as a race, their previous condition and associations are sufficient to account for the fact that their passions are ill-controlled; and that, among the more ignorant, the marriage tie is held in light esteem; that untruthfulness and dishonesty are, alas, too common, and that still more generally they are marked by a singular absence of any spirit of self-sacrifice for the general good. Now the establishment of well ordered and thoroughly trained sisterhoods among such a people is the lifting up of a standard of purity and self-sacrifice which cannot fail in time to do much toward correcting these very faults. This better type of life becomes familiar to them in the daily ministrations of the Sisters in their homes, in their instructions in school, in Bible classes and guild meetings, while the integrity of the life itself is protected by the rule, the mutual moral support, and above all by the life of prayer in the community.

This influence will be still greater when as in the case of the sisterhood we are now describing, women of their own race are admitted. So it has proved with the colored people. So it will doubtless be found to be in Africa, China, among the Indians, indeed among any people who need to be lifted to higher tone of life and morals.

CHAPTER VI.

OUR FAITHFUL DEPARTED.

Mount Calvary Church, which has taken so active a part in the defense of the Catholic practice of praying for the rest and refreshment of the faithful departed, has laid to rest, in the short space of eight years, three of her priests and two of the sisters working in the parish. Believing in the communion of saints, those who were left behind could not think that they would be forgotten in the prayers of those now brought nearer to God in the joys of Paradise. Their loss at the time, however, was grievous to bear, and the interruption of their earthly labors added to the many difficulties with which the work they loved has had to contend.

This record would seem cold indeed, did it omit to pay some tribute, however brief, to memories so dear and to labors so untiring.

The brave-hearted rector of Mount Calvary Church under whom was undertaken the work of S. Mary's, has already become known to the reader in the preceding chapters. His earnestness, his manliness, his devout tender spirit, fired by a zeal that might well in his case be called a consuming zeal, have doubtless already been recognized.

Joseph Richey was one who from early boyhood exercised a controlling influence over his companions and fellow-workers and drew to himself devoted friends and ardent admirers. His enthusiasm, his brilliant intellect, the positiveness of his convictions, were singularly blended with a woman's tenderness and sympathy. Men who widely differed from him respected him, and those who had keenly felt his reproofs, loved him.

Mr. Richey was born in Newry, County Down, Ireland, Oct. 5, 1843. From early childhood he was disciplined by severe trials. At the age of ten he was brought by his parents to the United States, and in 1859 he came to Baltimore to be educated under the care of his brother, the Rev. Dr. Thomas Richey, then rector of Mount Calvary Church. Later he was a student of S. Stephen's College, Annandale, and thence went to Trinity College, Hartford, where he graduated in 1866. In the General Theological Seminary, from which he graduated in 1869, the friendship between himself and the writer began. He was loved, respected and admired by his fellow-students, and took the position of a leader among them. His first parish was S. John's, Delhi, N. Y., and for a short time afterward he was assistant at the Church of the Advent, Boston, which was then under the charge of the Society of S. John the Evangelist. Thence he was called to the rectorship of Mount Calvary Church. The call to succeed Mr. Curtis presented as many difficulties as attractions, and Mr. Richey made a condition of his acceptance that his seminary friend should be associated with him in the responsibility of the rectorship. This was cordially agreed to by both bishop and vestry. The two young men began their work, and were soon joined by the Rev. Evelyn Bartow, who continued for nine years faithfully engaged in the work of Mount Calvary. It does not belong to this work even to briefly sketch Mr. Richey's short but eventful career. His monument is in the spiritual growth of the congregation, the daily celebration which he re-established with the promise of the bishop that it should not again during his episcopate be interrupted ; in the beautiful altar he erected ; in the work of the sisters whom he invited from England ; in the deep conviction with which his boldness, sincerity and sound learning caused many to grasp Catholic truth. These ends, however, were not accomplished without great wear and tear to a constitution which when he entered on his work seemed iron. When his co-laborers, as they saw his strength wane, suggested a diminution of labor, it resulted only in his taking a larger share himself, in order to relieve them. In addition to his pastoral duties, he undertook exhausting labors in a girls' school, the establishment of which, under the All Saints' Sisters, was the darling wish of his heart. In the midst of these labors came the presentment for trial for alleged erroneous teachings. He bravely bore the attack, but none the less the iron entered his soul and deeply wounded him. Great nervous strain was inevitable, even when the attack was confined to himself and his associate. When the bishop, because, as he said [Annual Address, Conv. Jour., 1875], he discovered in the articles charged, neither the offence of "advised teaching of doctrine contrary to that of this Church, nor the violation of ordination vows," refused to proceed to trial, and so brought the envenomed attack upon himself, Mr. Richey felt the bitterness of the situation most keenly. At length the strong constitution broke down. The congregation, with loving haste and lavish generosity, provided means for him to seek restoration to health in Europe. The journey, as Bishop Whittingham well expressed it in his address after Mr. Richey's death, proved to be "a vain effort for recuperation of faculties absolutely worn out by inordinate work."

He was passing up the Rhine toward Switzerland when his health failed rapidly and he turned back to England. He barely reached London in time to die. The end is thus described in a memorial sermon preached soon after his death by one who was his dear friend and for many years his spiritual father, the Rev. Dr. Brand:

"To the knowledge of all but himself he was dying when he reached London on the evening of the 17th of September, and yet he passed away unexpectedly. He had seen his one personal friend, Father Benson, in the evening. About six the loving mother of All Saints' Sisterhood left him, having been arranging with him that he should receive the Blessed Sacrament in the morning; at ten he sent word to her by a sister that he felt better. The Rev. Mr. Brinckman, chaplain to the All Saints' Sisters, who was in the same house, was with him as late as two in the morning, and then went down to his room, thinking that he was going on as usual; but at five he gave a deep sigh and passed away. This was on the morning of S. Matthew's Day." It was on S. Matthew's Day four years earlier that he blessed S. Mary's Chapel for its first service.

On S. Luke's Day, Oct. 18, 1877, that loved form lay in its oaken casket before the altar of Mount Calvary, where he had so dearly loved to celebrate. For him was pleaded that Eucharistic sacrifice which he had so often offered for others; at 7, 8, 9 and 10 o'clock at Mount Calvary, and at 6 and 7 at S. Mary's. At noon the order for the burial of the dead was said, and then the long procession—the longest funeral procession many thought that had ever passed through the streets of Baltimore—followed the sacred remains to S. John's churchyard at Waverly. The words of one who knew and loved him well, the Rev. Dr. Brand, in the sermon already quoted, may well conclude this tribute to his memory:

"In respect to all teaching and practice Mr. Richey was guided by his belief in one Catholic and Apostolic Church. In no respect had his theological principles changed since his ordination, and in all sincerity had he taken his vows which bound him to "minister the doctrine and sacraments and the discipline of Christ as this Church

10

hath received the same. Mr. Richey was emphatically of that school which calls itself Catholic.

"To the discipline of the Church enforced by
rightful authority, he unfeignedly submitted. I
was with him in attendance on the sessions of the
last general convention, when zeal burnt against
the 'ritualists' and the result of legislation was
feared. He at that time said to me, 'The convention can pass no canon that I am not ready fully
to obey.' He was a true and obedient son of the
Church, which is yet not wholly conformed to the
conceptions of one who cherished the life and
spirit of the earlier ages.

"His bold maintenance of his convictions and
his spirit of obedience to rightful rule were shown
by painful circumstances, which forced him to
meet manfully a notoriety from which his nature
shrank. I need not recall the facts, which are but
too fresh in your memory. The intended trial was
averted by your clergy rightly submitting to the
godly admonition of their bishop, and promising to
avoid what had been an occasion of stumbling; yet
without abandoning, and without being asked to
abandon, their conviction that, although not com-
manded in Holy Scripture, nor distinctly set forth
in our service book, commemoration of the faithful departed is legally observed in the English
Church, is clearly a primitive usage, and one familiar to, probably practiced by, our Lord and His
Apostles as Jews, certainly never condemned by
Him or them.

"You best know the faithfulness and loving nature of his private efforts to lead in the way of holiness.   Of his entire devotion to his work—his
Master's work—all are cognizant.   In labors he
was abundant.   Your clergy will tell you that,
while prompt to spare them, he never spared himself.   I myself have seen him later than two o'clock
taking his first morsel of food after constant labor
from six in the morning—a labor so wearying to
the body through the spirit—and this at a time
when the disease which cut short his days gave him
little rest in sleep.   And yet his complaint was
that he neglected duties.

' "One so faithful to others could not have been
negligent of his own soul.   I think he was tender
in his dealings with you.   I know that he was
severe in his judgment of himself.   He was as honest with himself as he was humble.   Save one who
long years ago left me to mourn, having at even a
much earlier age reached a wonderful spiritual development, he was of all men the most spiritual-
minded I have ever known."

Mr. Richey's place was very difficult to fill.
None but a single man could become the senior
priest of the clergy house, and rare gifts were required to minister to the much tried and now
deeply afflicted congregation.

No motives of delicacy would excuse the writer
from acknowledging the kindness of the vestry and
congregation in urging him to accept the vacant
rectorship.   The fear that the remembrance of his

friend would continually make him painfully conscious of his own inability to fill his place would of
itself have caused hesitation in accepting the call.
Other reasons strengthened his conviction that it
was his duty to decline it. It did not seem right
to abandon a peculiar missionary work to which he
had devoted himself, and especially at a time when
it might be hazardous to turn the work over to a
stranger unacquainted with its needs. He declined,
however, not without regret, especially as he fore-
saw that as the work at S. Mary's increased, the
opportunities of intercourse with friends he dearly
loved must grow less frequent. Generously appre-
ciating his motives, the vestry continued their kind
consideration for him, and extended the call to his
intimate friend, the present rector of Mount Calvary, the Rev. Robert Hitchcock Paine. Mr. Paine
had been formerly invited to join the work in Baltimore by his friend Mr. Richey. One may eulogize the
dead, but, of the living, good taste permits one only
to say that the writer has had reason to remain
grateful to the vestry for enabling him to thus re-
new a friendship of earlier years with him who,
with sympathy, untiring energy and kind consideration, has sustained all the efforts at S. Mary's in
addition to his faithful and arduous work at Mount
Calvary.

A previous chapter has related that the first to
join the clergy of Mount Calvary for the express
purpose of assisting in the work among the colored
people was the Rev. Alfred B. Leeson. He came, as

all the assistants in the work have come, immediately after graduating from the General Theological Seminary. He had been with us somewhat over a year when it was discovered that he was postponing his ordination to the priesthood because he had thought of joining the Church of Rome. The bishop was at once informed of the fact. On being pressed by him to receive priest's orders or to give his reason for delay, Mr. Leeson frankly acknowledged his doubts, resigned his position, and soon after made his submission to papal authority.

Nothing could have more seriously threatened injury to the work nor awakened more prejudice against it. The excitement over Mr. Curtis' secession from the Church had hardly subsided when this new trouble arose. It was found that Mr. Leeson had been in correspondence since his college days with Dr. Stone, a recent convert to Rome, and that friend's influence, and nothing connected with his life in Baltimore, prompted the step. But this did not prevent cruel suspicions and accusations of the work at S. Mary's. Mr. Leeson had been an indefatigable, earnest worker, and, as he deserved, the people were devotedly attached to him. The Sunday-school, the guilds and some other departments had been left wholly to his care. It would not have been strange had many followed him, especially among the younger people who had been more with him than with the other clergy. Yet neither then nor since his return to the city as one of an Order especially devoted to labor among the colored people (so far as is known), has a single one of S. Mary's communicants joined the Roman communion. In the meantime no inconsiderable number of Roman Catholics have been received at S. Mary's.

Fortunately at this very time a young relative of the priest in charge, the Rev. Oliver Perry Vinton, son of the Rev. Dr. Francis Vinton, of Trinity Church, New York, had been ordained, and having for some years evinced a lively interest in S. Mary's, was ready to decline tempting offers in order to join in its work. Mr. Vinton had graduated at S. Stephen's College, Annandale, in 1873, and at the General Theological Seminary in 1876, and had been ordained Deacon by Bishop Potter. Although never physically strong, he entered enthusiastically into his labors in Baltimore without any sparing of himself. The people soon became very much attached to him, a certain gentleness of disposition combined with great courtesy and refinement of manner, reached their hearts, and these gifts, with other advantages of birth and early training which would have made him an ornament in society, became the means of winning, Christianizing and elevating the humble people to whose welfare he consecrated these powers. Mr. Vinton, not content with his share of work at S. Mary's, longed to plant seed in some new field which he might watch and tend. Although it was feared, at the time, that his zeal outran his strength, one had not the heart to discourage such effort. A mission called,

at the bishop's request, Epiphany, was started in
South Baltimore. Many of the colored people of
that quarter of the city are very poor and ill-housed,
and nowhere are the ministrations of the Church
more needed. A small hall on Leadenhall Street
was rented. The site proved to be not well chosen.
The clergy lived too far away to conduct the work
effectually. The necessary aid in the way of money
and lay help could not be obtained. Mr. Vinton's
earnest efforts, therefore, were not rewarded with
much immediate success. This did not cool his
ardor. The less the response of the people the
greater his efforts ; until his spirit of sacrifice, his
patience and his gentleness began to win them.

Not infrequently when an evening meeting of
young men had been appointed, Mr. Vinton would
find that the sexton had forgotten to unlock the
door. He would get the key, and himself sweep
out the room and light the fire. At other times he
would patiently sit upon the steps, on several occasions in a drenching rain. Very often he waited
in vain for the expected guests (for engagements to
meet the colored people are most uncertain), and
would return at midnight to the clergy house pale,
weary and disheartened. A cold, taken on one of
these occasions, first revealed disease of his lungs.
Mr. Vinton's ardent, sanguine temperament did
not permit him readily to relinquish his work. As
neither rest nor medical skill succeeded in check-
ing the ravages of the disease, he at last went home
to his family in Pomfret, Conn., but only to die.

On the night of the 15th of June, 1880, he painlessly and peacefully passed away. At his own request, his body was brought to Baltimore to be placed by the side of his friend, Mr. Richey, whom he had greatly loved. After a celebration of the Holy Eucharist at S. Mary's, the bier, preceded by the choir and clergy chanting a solemn Miserere, was borne by S. Mary's Business Committee across the street to Mount Calvary. The choristers of Mount Calvary, and such clergy as had vested there, met the procession at the gate and proceeded into the church. The burial office was then said, and at the conclusion of the service a long funeral train composed of both Mount Calvary and S. Mary's choirs, and a large number of clergy, white and colored, friends and relatives, and a great many of both congregations, accompanied his remains to Waverly, where sorrowfully but hopefully he was laid to rest.

The work at South Baltimore was for a time carried on with great difficulty, but on the death of Mr. Vinton's successor, there being no assistant, it had to be abandoned. It would probably not have been resumed had not a lady of indomitable energy, Mrs. Robert C. Barry, asked that she might reopen the Sunday-school. Almost unaided by the clergy, who have been too busy to afford much help, she has gathered a Sunday-school of 125 scholars, and one day in the week has held a mothers' meeting of thirty women. A small tenement was rented on West Street, in the poorest and densest populated section, and the words "Vinton Memorial" were placed over the door. In every kind of weather this lady has been at her post of duty. Even during the winter, when small-pox was raging in that section of the city, although from the mission house seventeen yellow flags could be counted on the neighboring houses, the fear of disease did not keep her from her work. The grateful people might easily have been gathered, if proper provisions for them could have been made. We had hoped that long ere this some generous churchman would have given one of the many vacant lots of land in the neighborhood or the few hundred dollars needed for building a small chapel.

A year before Mr. Vinton's death, when it became evident that he had no longer strength to labor, another assistant was called. The Rev. Herbert Baring Smythe came, fresh from his seminary course. So full of enthusiasm was he, so blessed with physical strength and spirit, so devoted to his work from the very start, that it was hoped he would for many years brighten and lighten the burden now sorely pressing upon the shoulders of the other clergy. He had peculiar and rare gifts for the work. He did not know the meaning of discouragement. In his private life devout and almost austere, his manner with others had never a tinge of gloom, but was bright, sunny and cheery. Passionately fond of music and well skilled in its science, he never wearied in training the choristers, and he went in and out of the clergy house singing in rich, deep tones snatches of song like a happy bird. Full of sympathy and godly counsel for the mourner or the penitent, he was equally at home in merrymaking, and no pleasure excursion was considered complete without Mr. Smythe. The amount of work that he could press into a day was marvelous. When the writer, one night, noticing his weariness urged him to attempt less—"Why?" replied he brightly, "I am very tired each night, it is true, but why should I not be? I rest well and am ready for the same work the next day." When preparing classes for confirmation he would wait in his room till one o'clock at night for men employed till after midnight at hotels, and then, in his stocking-feet, that the other clergy might not be disturbed nor expostulate with him for "overwork," would slip down to the front door and let them in, and give them an hour's instruction. It has been the writer's privilege to live in daily intercourse with noble and earnest men. Some have fallen asleep; others are still left to him; but he thinks that he has never intimately known any one whose character, take it all in all, seemed to him so nearly perfect as Mr. Smythe's.

God saw fit that this noble soul should not be without trial in the furnace of affliction. One shadow fell over his happy life in Baltimore. The unending theological controversy in the diocese that has already so often appeared in these pages sought another victim. Without in any way being directed against Mr. Smythe personally—for he was hardly known to the members of the Standing Committee—the contest for a time centered upon him. His testimonials signed, as the Canon required them to be, by the clergy and vestry of Mount Calvary, were not accepted by the Standing Committee. Like other unwilling exiles from the Maryland Diocese, he was forced to seek ordination to the priesthood in a diocese of more liberal views. Cordially received by the Bishop of New York, he was ordained by him. The acrimony of the attack, and especially the wholly inexcusable hesitation in accepting his word—he was the soul of honor and frankness—wounded a deeply sensitive nature and seriously affected his health. The result will be stated in a short memoir furnished by the father he so dearly loved. Little did we think when we stood by the grave of Mr. Vinton with the elder Mr. Smythe, who was at the time visiting his son at our home, that in another year we should be sorrowing by his side over Herbert's grave. Very different from the great concourse of people at Waverly was the scene on that frontier of civilization where his father in missionary zeal had gone. Surrounded by a new congregation, who had known the son only through the loving description of his parents, but who showed the tenderest sympathy, the Holy Eucharist was celebrated on an extemporized altar in the place of worship, kindly loaned by the Presbyterians. Clad in his Eucharistic vestments, according to his dying request, he was laid to rest in the lonely prairie more than 1,000 miles from his Baltimore home. His body, now removed, lies beneath the shadow of a beautiful church in Canada. His father, at our request, has furnished the following brief memoir:

MEMOIR OF THE REV. H. B. SMYTHE, A. M.

Mr. Smythe was born in London, 27th of February, 1854, and was brought in childhood by his parents to this country, his father settling as Rector of S. John's Church, in Helena, Ark. From his earliest youth he aspired to the holy ministry of the Church, and from his first consciousness he corresponded with this aspiration, and looked forward to a life of service at God's altar. With that in mind, he kept himself pure and free from aught that might interfere with the fullest service he could render.

After a blameless boyhood, which endeared him to all who knew him, he entered Racine College in 1870, and graduated in 1876. Aided by the loving counsel of his revered instructor and adviser, the Rev. Dr. De Koven, he passed through all the departments of Racine, aiming to fit himself, with God's guidance, for his high calling. There, as at the General Theological Seminary, which he entered in 1876, he won for himself the love and respect of all his classmates and instructors, who looked for great blessings to the Church, from his steady perseverance, his entire consecration, his bright and amiable disposition, and his apparently strong and vigorous constitution.

Ready to give himself up to his chosen work, in the spring of 1879, his desire was to return with Bishop Schereschewsky to the China Mission, in regard to which the following memorandum is found on the fly-leaf of his pocket Bible: "April 17, Vigil of Maunday Thursday—to night I offered myself to the Bishop of China." He was hindered in this, however, by the delicate state of his mother's health.

Mr. Smythe was ordained to the diaconate June 15, 1879, at Christ Church, Croswell, Michigan. His father, being the rector, presented him to Bishop Gillespie, of Western Michigan, officiating. He at once entered on his work in Baltimore, where, in preference to many tempting offers elsewhere, including a call to be assistant minister at the Church of the Ascension, Chicago, he accepted a call to labor among the colored people in Baltimore, in the work carried on by the clergy of Mount Calvary Church.

Mr. Smythe was ordained priest in New York, by Bishop Potter, June 27, 1880. His father, the Rev. Wm. H. Smythe, preached the sermon, and assisted, with the clergy of Mount Calvary Church, Baltimore, and others of New York, in the services on that occasion.

Of his short ministry no adequate account can be given in this brief memoir. Those who were with him can alone testify of his labors in season

and out of season, and of symptoms which, all un-
consciously to them, as to him, began to weaken
and impair a vigorous and seemingly well-estab-
lished constitution. Circumstances and controversy, in no sense intended as personal, but which
centered to some extent in himself, made his entrance into the priesthood a time of trial and
perplexity, from the consequence of which Mr.
Smythe's timid and retiring nature had not recovered before, after a year of active service, God
took him to that Haven of Rest :

> " Where happier bowers than Eden's bloom,
>   Nor sin, nor sorrow know :
> Blest seat! through rude and stormy scenes
> I onward press to you."

These trials, borne with patience and fortitude,
served only to deepen the side of his devotional
character. The daily celebrations of Mount Calvary were his especial joy. Not one morning in
two years, as deacon and priest, did he fail to
attend the pleading of the one sacrifice, once
offered. One year of work in the priesthood and
his toil was over.

At the close of June, 1881, he left Baltimore for
a holiday, to which he had looked forward with
joyous anticipation, meaning to spend at least a
month with his loving parents, the Rev. Wm. H.
Smythe and wife, at Port Austin, Michigan. On
his way home he tarried for a few days with his
brother, E. H. Smythe, LL.D., at Kingston, Can-

ada. Here, however, he became conscious of the
presence of active disease ; but bearing up until
he could be nursed by a loving mother, he hastened
home. There, after a fortnight of seemingly
slight fever, his enfeebled frame was attacked with
acute peritonitis, and after a few hours of intense
suffering, in which his faith and trust never fal-
tered, sustained and comforted by the love of God,
extended through the sacraments of the Church,
and the indwelling of God the Holy Ghost, he
breathed back his soul to God who gave it, in the
arms of his loving mother, July 22, 1881.

This mournful fact was immediately telegraphed
to Baltimore, to the Rev. Robert H. Paine, Rector,
and the Rev. Calbraith B. Perry, associate Rector
of Mount Calvary Church, who immediately hastened with all speed to the chamber of death at
Port Austin. The funeral was performed, with
all due solemnity, by these loving companions in
labor. The Rev. Mr. Paine acted as celebrant at
the holy communion, and he and Mr. Perry made
affecting addresses on the solemn occasion.

There on the shores of Lake Huron were laid
away the remains of one whom all who had known,
loved, July 27, 1881. May he rest in peace, and
have a joyful rising in the day of Jesus Christ.

It might seem that the record of death were full.
Still more lives, however, were given to consecrate
this work. A year before Mr. Richey's departure,
we had knelt around the death-bed of one whose

life seemed scarcely less important to the work than that of the clergy. Sister Harriet had been sent out as Superior of the All Saints' Sisters in Baltimore, and for three years, with rare wisdom and great devotion, she had filled the position. It was during this time that, aided by her judgment and zeal, the colored Sisterhood was successfully begun. Sister Harriet had been one of the three postulants of the order at the time it was organized in London in 1856. She became noted in England as one whose sympathy and counsel were sought by every class in life. In America she maintained the same reputation, and when she was laid to rest (the first buried in the now well-filled lot at Waverly), she was followed to the grave by a great number of white and colored people, who sincerely mourned the loss of a friend who had soothed their sorrows and solved their perplexities. She entered into rest March 12, 1876. At the funeral services at Mount Calvary Church, twenty vested clergy in the choir showed their respect and their appreciation of her work, and the eighteen sisters present represented several religious orders. The Rev. Dr. Leeds, and the Rev. Messrs. Leakin, Wiley, Chipchase, Gibson, Cranston, Hobbie and Rose acted as pall-bearers, and the All Saints' school filled her grave with flowers. Sister Harriet's memory will be held ever dear in Baltimore, though the affectionate and generous care which the Rev. Mother in England has, from the first, bestowed on the American work, has made her loss felt as little as possible by the selection of her successor, and has supplied a number of other accomplished and devoted sisters for the work both of Mount Calvary and S. Mary's. Again death entered and took a very lovely character to her reward—Sister Mary Clement, the teacher of S. Mary's parish school. The girls under her care regarded her with the affection deserved and the respect inspired; although she well loved them and the work, she gladly accepted the release her Lord gave her from a lingering illness, and her grave is the fourth in the burial-lot at Waverly.

This tribute may be paid to the dead. Good taste forbids the same free expression of the living. Yet it must not be thought that there is no cause for thankfulness for their services. An earlier chapter has shown Mr. Bartow's interest and connection with the work. While two of the clergy of Mount Calvary have been more especially assigned to the work at S. Mary's, the other clergy have taken a deep interest, and frequent exchanges have been to the advantage of the congregation as well as a relief to themselves. Mr. Bartow continued to preach at S. Mary's twice a month, and when he accepted a call to a parish in New Jersey, he left many friends in S. Mary's, as well as a great number in Mount Calvary. His successor, the Rev. George Herbert Moffett, has aided from time to time in the schools, and it would only be necessary to mingle among the people to know how gladly they welcome him when his many

11

duties at Mount Calvary permit him to preach or otherwise assist at S. Mary's.

After Mr. Smythe's death, his place was temporarily filled by the Rev. Charles H. De Garmo. He spent only a winter with us, but he left a deep and lasting impression upon the congregation. Few, in so short a time, could have become so universally beloved, and it is another illustration of our assertion that those who are especially marked by gentleness of disposition and unusual courtesy of manner are peculiarly fitted to labor among the colored people.

The Rev. James Oswald Davis was our latest assistant. At the close of two years of faithful and earnest work, he has recently accepted a call to be assistant at the Church of S. Mary the Virgin, New York. He retired from the work from circumstances beyond control, regretted by clergy and congregation. During his stay he was particularly successful in the organization of several guilds and the more complete systematizing, under the sisters, of the care of the sanctuary and similar work.

It has been already intimated that the formation of guilds and societies among the colored people has not been found as fruitful as had been expected. This arises from the irregularity of members in performing duties and attending meetings, partly the result of the nature of their occupations and partly from their own peculiarities. Yet every means that tends to make them more

punctual or increase their sense of personal
responsibility should be employed, and the difficulties in keeping up their interest may be overcome. As a people, they are certainly fond of
forming societies, especially of such as have a great
number of officers or are employed largely in the
discussion of constitutions and by-laws. The
most popular societies among them are what are
known as "beneficial societies," which make provision for sickness and death among their members. When these have been honestly and wisely
conducted, they have done much to encourage
thrift and to prevent distress. Their odd and, it
must be allowed in some cases, somewhat grotesque
costumes or "regalia," as they appear in attendance at funerals, is somewhat startling to one
unaccustomed to them, while many of their names
are still more remarkable, as, for example, the
following, selected at haphazard from such as are
known to the writer: "Galilean Fishermen," "Be-
nevolent Daughters of Ebenezer," "Sons and
Daughters of Moses," "Freed Sons and Daughters
of Abraham Lincoln," "Sons and Daughters of
Jerusalem battling at the gate of Glory."

We have completed the list of our regular assistants.* Mr. Bishop's stay at S. Mary's was fully
treated in a previous chapter. Besides those mentioned who were canonically resident in the diocese,

---

* At the present time the Rev. Charles G. Maturin, late
curate of S. Barnabas, Pimlico, London, is, for a few months,
most earnestly and acceptably assisting in the work.

others, for a short time, have supplied vacant places, such as the Rev. George C. Street, whose kindly, genial ways will not be forgotten, and the Rev. J. B. Draper, who more recently, for some months, labored energetically at S. Mary's. These pleasant associations, with the occasional visits of Bishops and distinguished clergy, and the readiness of clergy of this and other dioceses to be present on festival occasions and to assist in times of need, have done much to cause the congregation to recognize the unity of the Church,* and to feel that, no longer outcasts, they are regarded with fraternal feeling and interest.

---

* As one of the most effectual means of uniting in Christian fellowship the two races should be mentioned the labors of those ladies who, with unwearying patience and faithfulness, have been fellow-workers of the colored teachers in the Sunday-schools and Day-schools.

CONCLUSION.

THE preceding chapters, which, it is feared, are somewhat disconnected and incomplete, have aimed not only to entertain those who have personal interest or association with the work recorded. In addition to this the writer has hoped to make some contribution, however trivial, towards the solution of a great problem which is before the Church. The solution itself he does not attempt; that is left to wiser heads. If he succeed in turning towards the subject the thoughts of those more competent to solve it, whose duty the Church makes it to at least attempt a solution, if he succeed in demonstrating the danger of delay, or furnish any information that affords encouragement or skill in grappling with it, his object will be accomplished.

The uplifting of a people freed from slavery and made citizens, likely forever to remain with us as such, and to increase and not decrease in numbers, is of the utmost importance and brooks no dallying.* There has been no attempt to conceal the

---

* The last pages of this work were in press before the writer had read Judge Tourgee's last book, "Appeal to Cæsar," the most thoughtful treatise on the "Negro Problem" that has yet appeared. Had the book been met earlier, some of its startling statistics and irresistible conclusions drawn from them, would have been quoted to enforce the writer's own appeal to Churchmen to render unto

difficulties of the task. That a great portion of the colored people are living in dense ignorance and in sin, cannot be denied. But it has been the object of the preceding pages to prove:

First, that great as are the evils, they have been exaggerated. They are by no means universal. The exceptions—exceptions very marked, and increasing under favorable circumstances, are a guarantee of the possibility of altogether eradicating them.

Secondly, that the evils are not inherent and necessary characteristics of the negro race as such. They are not "native traits." They are largely the result of the white man's dealing with the black; it follows that it is his duty to undo the evils he has done.

Thirdly, that the Church can overcome these evils. It has been a chief object of this book to present actual cases in which the Church has done so. Moreover, the victory has been gained amid opposition and complications in nowise necessarily connected with this special work, but springing

---

God "the things that are God's," no less than they are things which affect the welfare of Cæsar. No Christian ought—more than any patriot or legislator—to neglect a careful study of the facts which the author of "Appeal to Cæsar" presents. Those most prejudiced against his former works will acknowledge his fairness and breadth of sympathy in his treatment of these facts. The book will form a valuable hand-book of necessary information and useful suggestions to all engaged in any department of work among the colored people.

from local and temporary causes. Such difficulties need not therefore be taken into account in estimating the chances of success elsewhere.

No attempt has been made to conceal difficulties. They arise chiefly from the apathy and unreasonableness of the North, the sensitiveness, prejudice, and theorizing of the South, the ignorance, the self-indulgence and indolence of the colored people themselves, and the unwillingness of all three to unite in the sacrifice necessary to accomplish the end in view. These are difficulties that can be overcome, and ought to be. The barriers are not insurmountable.

Can Christian men long remain indifferent if the Church faithfully and persistently presents the case to them? Those who have loudly insisted on the unity of the nation, which necessarily implies unity and community of interest, must see the vital importance not only to those who live in closest proximity to the danger but to the whole land, of purifying and enlightening this element of our civilization. At least let the Church, so long as her offerings for her conversion remain the miserable pittance that they now are, abstain from boasting of her eagerness to open her arms to the colored man. Does the declaration publicly made that the North is ready to supply the means when the South has devised the way represent any honest sentiment in the North? The "Sewanee Conference" proposed a plan and asked for legislation from the last General Convention, 1883. The special

legislation asked for was deemed unwise. It needed important modifications. Granted; we think so.
But could not some better way have been substituted? Is it not as important that the Grace of
the Sacraments committed to the Church should
be dispensed to these five millions of people as that
the form of words in which the Sacraments are administered should be enriched? Was the response
that "the Board of Managers for Domestic and
Foreign Missions be requested to appropriate the
sum of $50,000 per annum for work among the
Colored People" mere irony? If to devise a plan
was not the business of the legislative body, as
was claimed by some, was it not of the Board of
Missions? Is it not somebody's business? A
joint resolution of both Houses declared that
the work of the Church among the Colored
People "ought to receive a large share of the
cares and benefactions of our Board of Missions."
How large a share of care it may receive the Board
of Managers alone can testify. That it does not
receive a large share of the benefactions is abun-
dantly shown by their reports. We asked bread;
they gave us a stone.

But all this does not excuse those Dioceses in
which are found the largest number of the colored
people, from earnestly prosecuting the work. Let
the cry that the South is too poor to do so be raised
no longer. It is sheer nonsense. That the means
and men at the disposal of the Church of the South,
or indeed of the whole Church, are not commensu-

rate with the work to be done, is most true. Insignificant indeed are the offerings of all Christendom for converting the Chinese Empire. Yet we keep a Bishop and a little staff of missionaries as a spark of Gospel light on the face of that vast realm. The South is not too poor to make a beginning. Undoubtedly parts of the South are poor. But is Baltimore poor? Is Richmond poor? Is New Orleans or Charleston or St. Louis? Are they so destitute of fine churches or wealthy laymen that there cannot be one properly sustained work among the colored people in any of them?—one church hospital or charity of any kind, one educational institution at all worthy of the Church? Why talk about what they cannot do, when they have not done what they can? It is not so much the means that is lacking as it is the will.

Doubtless the manner of working will have to be mended and modified to suit the necessities of the case. Prejudice must bend before duty. The Church at the South must be ready to learn as well as to instruct, to receive suggestions as well as to make them. We should be loath to believe that Dr. Tucker speaks for the whole Church in the South when he says, "When Northern Christians of any name propose to help the negroes, the Southern Christians draw back with a feeling of despair mingled with anger;" or that his exhortation "Send no Northern missionaries down here" would meet general indorsement. Does he confound his brethren in the priesthood with "carpet-bag" politicians! Such language is preposterous and does vast injury to the cause. More than one can testify that "Northern men, proposing to help the negro," have met a hearty welcome and God-speed from many thoroughly representative men of the South. When the opposite feeling exists, and in some quarters it does exist, it had best be ignored and allowed to die with as little attention called to it as possible.

The magnitude of the work, its difficulties, its many-sided aspects, demand the offerings, the wisdom, and the willing personal co-operation of all sections of the country and of both races. Let the results of experience be gathered from all quarters, both within and without the Church, and then let her wisest counselors, white and black, representing all parts of the country, unite with singleness of heart and purpose to deduce from the evidence before them the surest methods of success. Guided by their counsel, let the Church go forth, in harmony and in strength, to the work, and let the willing laborer be welcomed without asking whence he comes or what the color of his skin.

The colored people must do their share of bending to the needs. They too must conquer prejudice, hardly less strong even in regard to color lines among themselves than the prejudices of the whites. They must be ready to respond to efforts made in their behalf, and must sustain them whether made by representatives of their own race or by others. If a bishop bravely stands

forth for ecclesiastical rights of colored church
men, as the Bishop of South Carolina seems to
have done, his action should receive generous recognition not only—as it has—from the estimable
congregation which he championed, but from the
colored people everywhere. They must hold up the
hands of those who do labor for them, or who in
their behalf brave public sentiment ; otherwise few
will be encouraged to add themselves to the number. They must be no less patient with prejudices
which are natural to the former master than they
are with traits which are characteristics of the former slave. They must cease grumbling and repin-
ing over the want of advantages which, however,
they may manfully seek by all legitimate means,
while they must make the best of the ones which
they have. They must cease to regard themselves
with indolent and contented self-complacency, to
expend their best energies in idle self-vindication,
lest it be said of them as of those Corinthians
of old who " commended themselves," that they
" measuring themselves by themselves and compar-
ing themselves among themselves are not wise."
That the negro should have been driven into this
unfortunate frame of mind is not strange. As a
recent writer among themselves has truly said,
" He has been made the victim of the most exalted
panegyric by one set of fanatics, and of the most
painful, malignant abuse and detraction by another
set. The one has painted him as a sort of angel,
and the other as a sort of devil ; when in fact he

is neither one nor the other; when simply he is a *man*, a member of the common family possessing no more virtue nor vice than his brother."

But this same author, Mr. T. Thomas Fortune, who is a prominent and clever leader among his people, and whose book "*Black and White*" contains much that is marked by shrewd common sense, seems to cast a slur upon Christian labors among his people. He apparently places all hope of their progress upon secular education and material prosperity. It is a symptom of a dangerous sentiment spreading among their most intelligent class. This tendency doubtless finds its cause, though not its justification, in the very imperfect way that Christianity has been presented to them. The tendency is natural, but none the less pernicious.

The difficulties we have enumerated face the Church. None of them are invincible. For victory our Church is furnished with weapons which, we believe, no other religious body, no other moral agency, possesses. Let her but enter the field bravely, fearlessly, with energy and with self-sacrifice, and the victory is assured. As for mere social questions, as another has wisely said, the best way of dealing with them is to ignore them. The Church has nothing to do with them. They will take care of themselves. Neither can the colored people extend purely social privileges by legislation, nor the whites so restrict them. Social relations are regulated by laws not subject to human control. In her own sphere the Church has her canon of Christian charity imposed by Him who is no respecter of persons; unmoved by worldly considerations, let her do what is right and leave consequences to God.

With these objects in view, the writer trusts he may be pardoned for having so long tried the patience of his readers; and in closing his book, he would make his own the beautiful prayer uttered in Westminster Abbey by that able and worthy representative of the negro race, the Bishop of Hayti:

"O Thou Saviour Christ, Son of the Living God, who when Thou wast spurned by the Jews of the race of Shem, and who, when delivered up without cause by the Romans of the race of Japheth, on the day of Thy ignominious crucifixion, hadst Thy ponderous cross borne to Golgotha's summit on the stalwart shoulders of Simon the Cyrenian, of the race of Ham, I pray Thee, O Precious Saviour, remember that forlorn, despised, and rejected race, whose son thus bore Thy cross, when Thou shalt come in the power and majesty of Thy eternal Kingdom to distribute Thy crowns of everlasting glory!

"And give to me then, not a place at Thy right hand or at Thy left, but only the place of a gatekeeper at the entrance of the Holy city, the new Jerusalem, that I may behold my redeemed brethren, the saved of the Lord, entering therein to be partakers with Abraham, Isaac, and Jacob of all the joys of Thy glorious and everlasting Kingdom!"

NOTE.—While these pages were passing through the press a letter—upon quite another subject—was received from the Rt. Rev. Dr. Holly containing the following gratifying sentences : "I am glad to say we find Alice to be all that our fondest hopes could have pictured to our imagination. Many thanks for this most substantial service that you and your worthy co-laborers have thus rendered to the poor, struggling Church in Hayti." May God continue to bless the work of Alice and of her noble, self-sacrificing Bishop. A Philadelphia paper has also recently announced that Mr. James G. Davis, the former pupil of S. Mary's, whose creditable course in Philadelphia has been alluded to, has by competitive examination won the first honor in his class at the Franklin Institute, and in consequence has been assigned the work of preparing the drawing of a steam engine for the annual Exhibition.